A HEART OF STONE

Vanora clapped her hands together.

"That is brilliant of you, my Lord, and now I don't feel so afraid."

"That is something I have no wish for you to feel and thank you again for being so wonderful."

He bent forward and to her astonishment kissed her cheek.

It was only a light kiss, but, as his lips touched her skin, she felt a little quiver go through her.

The Earl walked away without looking back and she stood watching him until he was out of sight.

Only as she went into her bedroom did she put her hand to her cheek.

How amazing it was.

He had kissed her!

She had come to The Castle to carry out Ewen's orders and never had she dreamt for a single moment that she would be in any way intimate with the Earl.

Or that he would treat her as he would treat a woman in the same Social world as himself.

She was just an employee.

THE BARBARA CARTLAND
PINK COLLECTION

Titles in this series

A HEART OF STONE

BARBARA CARTLAND

Barbaracartland.com Ltd

THE BARBARA CARTLAND PINK COLLECTION

Dame Barbara Cartland is still regarded as the most prolific bestselling author in the history of the world.

In her lifetime she was frequently in the Guinness Book of Records for writing more books than any other living author.

Her most amazing literary feat was to double her output from 10 books a year to over 20 books a year when she was 77 to meet the huge demand.

She went on writing continuously at this rate for 20 years and wrote her very last book at the age of 97, thus completing an incredible 400 books between the ages of 77 and 97.

Her publishers finally could not keep up with this phenomenal output, so at her death in 2000 she left behind an amazing 160 unpublished manuscripts, something that no other author has ever achieved.

Barbara's son, Ian McCorquodale, together with his daughter Iona, felt that it was their sacred duty to publish all these titles for Barbara's millions of admirers all over the world who so love her wonderful romances.

So in 2004 they started publishing the 160 brand new Barbara Cartlands as *The Barbara Cartland Pink Collection*, as Barbara's favourite colour was always pink – and yet more pink!

The Barbara Cartland Pink Collection is published monthly exclusively by Barbaracartland.com and the books are numbered in sequence from 1 to 160.

Enjoy receiving a brand new Barbara Cartland book each month by taking out an annual subscription to the Pink Collection, or purchase the books individually.

The Pink Collection is available from the Barbara Cartland website www.barbaracartland.com via mail order and through all good bookshops.

In addition Ian and Iona are proud to announce that The Barbara Cartland Pink Collection is now available in ebook format as from Valentine's Day 2011.

For more information, please contact us at:

Barbaracartland.com Ltd.
Camfield Place
Hatfield
Hertfordshire AL9 6JE
United Kingdom

Telephone: +44 (0)1707 642629
Fax: +44 (0)1707 663041
Email: info@barbaracartland.com

THE LATE DAME BARBARA CARTLAND

Barbara Cartland who sadly died in May 2000 at the age of nearly 99 was the world's most famous romantic novelist who wrote 723 books in her lifetime with worldwide sales of over 1 billion copies and her books were translated into 36 different languages.

As well as romantic novels, she wrote historical biographies, 6 autobiographies, theatrical plays, books of advice on life, love, vitamins and cookery. She also found time to be a political speaker and television and radio personality.

She wrote her first book at the age of 21 and this was called *Jigsaw*. It became an immediate bestseller and sold 100,000 copies in hardback and was translated into 6 different languages. She wrote continuously throughout her life, writing bestsellers for an astonishing 76 years. Her books have always been immensely popular in the United States, where in 1976 her current books were at numbers 1 & 2 in the B. Dalton bestsellers list, a feat never achieved before or since by any author.

Barbara Cartland became a legend in her own lifetime and will be best remembered for her wonderful romantic novels, so loved by her millions of readers throughout the world.

Her books will always be treasured for their moral message, her pure and innocent heroines, her good looking and dashing heroes and above all her belief that the power of love is more important than anything else in everyone's life.

"There is only one cure for a heart of stone and that is love and even more love."

Barbara Cartland

CHAPTER ONE
1824

Vanora McKyle was standing very still on the deck of the small ship that was sailing towards the North.

She was thinking, as she had often mused before, that nothing in the world could be more beautiful than the moors of Scotland when they were purple with heather and the lights were different from those of any other place she had ever seen.

She had so far had a very interesting voyage from England.

She had not been intending to come home yet to Scotland, as she had been happy living with her uncle in London and helping him with the book that he was writing.

Very unexpectedly her brother, the Chieftain of the McKyle Clan, had insisted that she should return home.

Vanora's mother had died when she was not quite seventeen.

Her parents had been talking about how she should finish her education and the far North of Scotland was not the place to find Tutors or schools that would teach her what she wanted to learn.

Vanora's mother had been a relation of the Duke of Buccleugh, one of the richest Dukes who owned more land in Scotland than any of the others.

Her brother, for many years, had been the Secretary of State for Scotland and he had, on his retirement, been made Lord Blairmond.

When he heard his sister had died, Lord Blairmond invited Vanora to come to London and suggested that she should stay with him and attend a Finishing School, which was what her mother had always wanted for her.

Her father agreed and Vanora had gone to London and she was excited at moving into a world she had never seen before but had heard so much about.

Her uncle had greatly enjoyed her company. He had never married and so he was somewhat lonely.

He also, as time passed, found Vanora so intelligent that she could help him with a book he was writing about his years as Secretary of State for Scotland.

He owned a large library and Vanora found herself absorbed not only in the books he wanted her to research but also in those she chose for herself.

She was, in fact, very happy with her uncle and it never occurred to her to want to return to Scotland.

Then unexpectedly so that it was like a sharp blow, her father died suddenly of a heart attack.

This meant that her brother Ewen became Chieftain of the McKyle Clan.

*

Six months after he had taken up this responsibility, he sent for Vanora.

"I really cannot understand it, Uncle Angus," she said, "why Ewen wants me to return. After all he must be very busy with the Clan. He always had different ideas from Papa's and will now be putting them into action."

"I shall indeed miss you, my dear," Lord Blairmond replied, "but I think that you ought to go. If ever you want to return, you know that I shall be waiting for you eagerly."

Vanora was almost in tears when she left.

She had spent nearly three years in London and had made a great many friends. And it was an effort to turn her back on them and return to Scotland.

By a lucky chance a close friend of Lord Blairmond was going to Edinburgh in his yacht and he offered to take Vanora with him, which made the first part of the journey very pleasant, but she only wished that she had time to see Edinburgh.

She had read a great deal about the famous City when King George IV had visited Scotland for the first time two years earlier when he had received an enthusiastic reception which surprised everyone.

'If I cannot go and see Edinburgh now,' Vanora told herself, 'perhaps I will be able to do so later. I cannot imagine that I shall find a great deal to do except sit by the River Aulay and watch Ewen fishing.'

Lord Blairmond's friend had found her a passage on a ship from Edinburgh to John O'Groats. It had none of the comforts that Vanora had enjoyed on the yacht, but she was a good sailor and enjoyed being at sea.

She was able to gaze out at the glorious coastline of Scotland all the time they sailed North.

The Aulay was the river on her brother's estate and it ended in a fishing village by the sea called Aulaypool.

Vanora learned from the Captain that he invariably called in there and so there would be no difficulty in her disembarking when they arrived.

On arrival she found her brother's servants waiting for her at the harbour with a carriage drawn by two horses.

She had, just before the ship arrived at Aulaypool, been entranced as they passed the bay where standing out majestically was Killdona Castle.

Ever since she had been small she had heard about Killdona Castle and had longed to see it.

But this had been impossible.

An age-old feud had existed for a great many years between the McKyles and the Earl of Glenfile who owned The Castle.

For centuries the McKyles and the MacFiles had intermittently fought each other.

Neither of them had been able to claim an outright victory until fifteen years ago when the old Earl of Glenfile finally routed the McKyles having claimed that they were stealing his sheep.

Whether that was the truth or not, the battle was fierce and bloody and a great number of men on both sides were wounded and it seemed almost a miracle that not a single man was actually killed.

It was then that the Earl had declared himself the victor and told the McKyles that, if they could not behave in future, he would sweep them off the face of the earth!

Vanora had been only a small child at the time and could recall little of what had happened.

She had, in fact, been protected by hiding in one of the caves in the Strath with her mother and a Nanny and there they had been safe until the battle was over.

Her father was furious at being defeated, but there had been nothing he could do.

The Earl of Glenfile had not only a much larger Clan under his command but he was a larger landowner and very much richer.

Vanora had always heard it said that 'a Scot never forgets' and that was certainly true where the McKyles were concerned.

She could not remember as she grew older ever dining with her father without his raising his glass to drink a toast to the damnation and utter destruction of the Earl of Glenfile and those who followed him.

She mused as the ship sailed past Killdona Castle that nothing could look more romantic or more attractive.

It had been restored and renovated several times since it was first built and in the last century tall towers had been added that gave it a very picturesque appearance.

Some way above sea level was a nicely laid-out garden that led directly down to the bay.

'I do wish I could visit The Castle and see inside it,' Vanora reflected.

But she knew that, in the circumstances of the feud, it was something that would never happen, so it was no use wishing for the moon.

Instead, as they drove away from the little harbour, she told herself that she was happy to be home.

It would be exciting to be back in their own castle, which was actually older than Killdona.

Her mother had told her legends and Fairy stories about it ever since she was old enough to understand and it would have been impossible for any Scot not to be proud of such an illustrious history.

At one time the McKyle Clan had owned far more land and were of great standing with whatever Scottish King was reigning at the time.

Yet gradually they had preferred to stay on their own land and leave the political world to look after itself and, by the time Vanora's father became the Chieftain, he was content with making sure the lambing went smoothly and, if they were not exactly rich, that no one was in want.

As the horses carried her up the Strath, she could see that the River Aulay was fairly high and this meant that the fishing would be good and so plenty of salmon to eat.

When she first saw the McKyle Castle tower, she felt a little thrill of excitement go through her.

She was home!

Even though she would miss her mother and father, Ewen was there and she would be among her kith and kin.

He was waiting for her at the front door and she felt he looked a little older than when she had last seen him.

"You have come!" he exclaimed, "I was frightened, after all I had written, that you would refuse me."

"You were so insistent that, of course, I could not say 'no' and here I am."

He laughed and they walked inside together.

It was just as she had remembered it, perhaps just a little more austere and lacking in the feminine touch her mother had always given it.

They went up the stairs to the drawing room which as usual in Scotland was on the first floor.

Tea was waiting for her by the fireside and she poured out a cup for her brother.

"Now tell me what is happening?" she asked him. "The way you wrote made me very apprehensive in case something terrible has overcome you."

"Nothing bad," he replied, "but I need your help."

"Of course I will do anything I can, Ewen."

She nearly added that it had better be something very important as her uncle was annoyed that she should be leaving him when he had not yet finished his book.

Now, as she was waiting for her brother to speak, she was aware that he was looking a little strange.

It was as if he found it difficult to tell her what was on his mind.

"Come on, Ewen," she urged, "what is the secret? Are you to be married or something equally dramatic?"

"No, nothing like that and I have no intention of getting married or of producing an heir until I have set my people back in the place they are entitled to."

"What do you mean by that?" she asked.

"I mean to make the McKyles as significant as they surely were in my grandfather's and great-grandfather's day. That, as you know, was before we were humiliated by the Earl of Glenfile."

Vanora sighed.

"Oh, not that old story again, Ewen! I am sick and tired of hearing how he beat us up. If you ask my opinion, I think he had good reason to do so. From what I heard, the McKyles were stealing his sheep!"

"I don't know who you have been listening to," her brother said sharply, "but that is a lie that I am determined to rebut. Now the first thing I want back is our Stone."

Vanora stared at him.

"Our Stone!" she exclaimed.

She had heard the story so often, but had never thought it of any great consequence.

When the MacFiles had defeated the McKyles, the Earl had taken away from them the Stone the Chieftain of the Clan was always seated on to be proclaimed Chieftain.

The McKyles had adopted the old custom set by the 'Stone of Scone' on which all the Scottish Kings were crowned until it was removed to Westminster Abbey by Edward I.

During her researches for her uncle, Vanora had been interested in the stories about the Stone of Scone.

She had learned that in accordance with the custom of his ancestors, the King of Scotland was not crowned at the beginning of his reign and he was later 'set upon the Stone' which was at Scone.

The Stone was alleged to have accompanied the Scots on their mythical journeying and it had a great appeal to them with their inborn fey and vivid imagination.

The old Stone of Scone foretold that '*wherever the Stone should rest a King of Scots would reign.*'

After the stories about the Stone and the very strong feelings the Scots had for it, she found one aspect rather disappointing.

It was to learn that the Stone in Westminster Abbey was of a coarse-grained sandstone, fitted at each side with iron staples and rings for carrying it, although these might have been added by Edward I.

The McKyle Stone, that had been with the Clan all down the centuries, was of marble.

It was not very deep, but was wide enough to be set on the chair on which the Chieftain sat when he received the loyal allegiance of his people.

One by one the members of the Clan approached him dressed in his great finery as Chieftain. They knelt before him and kissed the ring on his left hand and then they swore obedience to him in life and in death.

Vanora thought it sad that she had not been present when Ewen had taken his father's place.

It was obvious, she now remembered, that it had been impossible for him to sit on the Stone as the Earl of Glenfile had taken it away when he defeated the McKyles.

"In future," he had said spitefully, "your Chieftain will never again have the authority you have given him, as he cannot accept it sitting on the Stone which is his throne. So he will not have the blessing of other Chieftains as he has lost what is, to all intents and purposes, his crown."

Vanora had always thought it was unkind of him to rub in so unpleasantly the fact that he had been victorious.

But what was done was done and surely it was no use Ewen thinking now that he could take it back.

As if he followed her thoughts, Ewen said,

"Do you think I am not aware when I go amongst other Chieftains that they are sniggering at me because I lost the Stone that gave my ancestors the esteem they were held in all over Scotland?"

"Surely they have stopped thinking about it after so many years," Vanora said. "Besides most Chieftains don't have a Stone or anything like it."

"Which is why they are not as important as we were before Glenfile stole it from us."

The way Ewen spoke told her all too clearly that the Stone meant as much to him as it had to their father.

Her mother had always told her how bitterly her father had resented the Earl stealing the Stone from them.

Aloud Vanora said,

"It has gone, Ewen, and there is nothing we can do to take it back. It would most certainly be a mistake to challenge the new Earl in any way."

She had learned when she was in England that the old Earl was dead and that his son, Viscount File, was now the tenth Earl of Glenfile.

She had been interested as he was their neighbour and she had learned from the newspapers that he had been educated in Edinburgh and had then gone on to Oxford.

Since he had grown up, much of his time had been spent in England.

He had joined up with the Regiment of the Argyll and Sutherland Highlanders, but, when the war with the French was over, he was not sent abroad.

Vanora had seen his name in *The Court Circular*, which reported all the smart balls and Receptions given by the King and the fashionable hostesses in London.

Then when he had come into his father's title, there was a certain amount written about him in the newspapers.

It seemed, she thought, rather unnecessary, but, if Ewen was determined to beg the new Earl to return the Stone, nothing would stop him.

"What are you going to do," she asked, "if the Earl refuses to give you back the Stone when you ask for it?"

Her brother stared at her.

"You don't really think," he said, "that I intend to go down on my knees and ask the Earl to snub me, as he would undoubtedly do?"

Vanora looked surprised.

"So, if you are not going to ask him for the Stone, how do you intend to get it back?"

"That is where *you* come in, Vanora."

"I don't understand what you mean."

"That is why I have brought you back here, my dear sister, to tell you what I want you to do."

Vanora looked at him apprehensively.

She knew that her brother had always had a very strong will. In fact her mother had often said that it was impossible to restrain him from doing what he wanted.

There was a determination about him that was good in a Clan Chieftain, but it did not, Vanora mused, make him easy to live with.

If Ewen wanted something, he demanded it and it was very difficult to refuse him.

"What I have already done," Ewen said, "is to send particulars of you to his Lordship."

"Particulars of me! What have you done that for?"

"I discovered that they are looking for a librarian and are intending to advertise for one in the newspapers."

"*A librarian*? You cannot be suggesting – "

"That is just what I am suggesting," he interrupted. "But you will not go to their castle as Vanora McKyle, because in the first place the Earl would not have you and, in the second, I have no wish for anyone to know what we are doing."

"Are you seriously proposing that I should become a librarian to the Earl? For what reason?"

"That is the first sensible thing you have said so far," her brother replied. "The reason, my dear sister, is obvious. You will find and bring back here the Stone of the McKyles and it will once more be in our possession."

Vanora drew in her breath.

"But I could not do it," she retorted. "I have no intention of stealing anything from anyone."

"It is not stealing, it is taking back what belongs to us in the first place. No one could ever pretend for a second that the Stone, which has been in the possession of the McKyles for four hundred years could belong to the MacFiles or was stolen unlawfully, in fact it was a criminal offence."

"Two wrongs don't make a right," Vanora insisted. "If I bring it back for you, provided I am not caught and imprisoned as a thief, you will have behaved no better than the Earl did in the first place in taking it from us."

Ewen's lips tightened.

"I have every intention of taking what is mine. It is something I need myself and wish to leave it for my heirs so that they will use it and in turn the next generations will do so into infinity."

"That sounds very like you," Vanora said. "At the same time it is something I cannot do for you. I am sorry Ewen, but you have brought me back here under false pretences."

There was silence before her brother asserted,

"You will do what I tell you, because I am your Chieftain. If you refuse, I will *exile* you from the Clan."

Vanora stared at him.

She could not believe what she had just heard.

She had once, seven years ago, seen a man exiled from the Clan after her father had warned him again and again to behave himself.

Then he had been found raping a woman who was too weak to resist him and she was the wife of another Clansman.

He had been exiled in front of the whole Clan and Vanora would never forget the look of despair on his face even though he was debauched. He had turned and walked away, knowing he had to leave McKyle land before dark.

She had not understood at the time exactly what the man had done and she was too young and innocent to be informed. But she had felt worried for him, although she knew that what he had done must have been wrong.

She realised that she just could not face it if Ewen carried out his threat to banish her publicly.

"You are trying to intimidate me," she said, "and I refuse to be intimidated."

"You must obey me, Vanora, and I am not speaking lightly when say that, if you don't, I shall punish you."

"How can I possibly do what you ask, Ewen?"

"It will be quite simple and, of course, I shall help you in every possible way."

She did not speak and he went on,

"So you will go to Killdona Castle tomorrow. The Earl has already received all your particulars and a strong recommendation of how experienced you are as a librarian, signed by your uncle."

"How could you have that?" Vanora asked.

"I fortunately have letters from our uncle and so I was able to copy his signature quite easily," Ewen replied. "And I think you will be quite impressed by what he says about you. After all he has always praised you in every letter he has written to me and found you indispensable."

That was true and Vanora could not deny it.

Then she asked,

"If, purely because I cannot help it, I apply for this position and get it, what am I to do?"

"You will find out first where the Stone is kept. I have a suspicion that it is on show, so that visitors can see how clever the late Earl was in defeating our people and humiliating them."

There was a note in his voice that told her only too clearly how much this affected him.

She wanted to scream that she could not do such a thing and if necessary she would go down on her knees to beg Ewen not to make her do it.

Yet she knew quite well that it was useless and he was not going to listen to anything she said.

Having made up his mind, as he had done all his life, he would surely get his own way.

Quickly, because it was the first thing that came into her head, she said,

"Will the Earl not think it strange that someone from this Clan, who he knows hates him, is applying for a position at Killdona Castle?"

Ewen gave a laugh that had no humour in it.

"Surely you don't think me as stupid as all that? Of course you will not go as yourself. You will go as a young woman from England, who has friends in Scotland with whom she is staying."

He paused before he went on,

"When she saw the advertisement in the newspaper, she thought it might be more interesting than the work she was doing at the moment."

Vanora did not reply and he went on proudly,

"I have covered my tracks very carefully, or rather your tracks. I wrote to the Earl from a hotel in Edinburgh when I was there a week or so ago. I managed to erase a few words you had written on your uncle's writing paper when you had sent me a book. So your reference is on Lord Blairmond's writing paper and signed by him."

Vanora did not know what to say. She only knew that every instinct in her body cried out at having to act out such a deception.

How could she do anything so difficult as to steal back the Stone of the McKyles?

She could not, however, pretend not to realise how much it meant to her brother, just as it had to her father.

It was a treasure they revered and to them it was more precious than anything else they owned.

"If I do this," she said after what seemed a long and poignant silence, "how can I take it away from Killdona Castle?"

"I promise you that I have thought out every danger and every trap that you might fall into by mistake. Once you are inside The Castle, I will have a man pick up any information you may wish to send me from a place on the edge of the garden."

Vanora gave a little shiver as it all seemed to her very frightening.

"Maybe his Lordship will not engage me – "

She knew as she spoke that it was something she was praying would happen.

Her brother smiled a little unpleasantly.

"He has already asked you to go for an interview tomorrow afternoon."

"If he did not send the letter here, where did he send it?" Vanora quizzed him.

"You are supposed to be staying with some friends of mine, the Rosses," Ewen replied. "As you know, they are not of our Clan, but they have always lived in the house on the side of the hill."

"Have you told them what I am doing?"

"No, of course not," he said scornfully. "I am not as stupid as that. I have only told them that there will be a letter addressed to Miss Bruce who is staying with us, but did not wish the Earl to be aware of it, knowing the feud between us."

Vanora could not help thinking it was rather clever of him, but she had no intention of saying so.

She merely rose and walked to the window.

She gazed out at the garden sloping down through the trees to the river and there was also a wonderful view of the hills rising on the other side of the Strath.

It all seemed so beautiful and so peaceful and she could hardly imagine how she could have possibly stepped into what seemed to her a hornet's nest.

Her brother drew a letter from his pocket.

"This is from his Lordship's secretary. He thanks you for your letter and says his Lordship will be pleased to see you at three o'clock tomorrow afternoon."

"What am I to say to him?" Vanora asked.

"Very little," her brother replied. "I have already given him a most graphic account of your experience in London and your uncle has written effusively as to how clever you are and how brilliantly you have attended to his library."

"As the Earl has just come into the title," Vanora suggested in a last desperate effort to save herself, "surely it would be worthwhile to ask him first if he would let bygones be bygones. He might easily give you back the Stone without all this fuss and commotion about it."

"And if he refuses, as doubtless he would, we would never have another chance like this. He would be suspicious of anyone who attempted to gain access to his castle, however well-disguised."

He walked towards her before he added,

"And I am certain that, like his father, he wants to keep the McKyles crushed under his feet and admitting his supremacy."

Vanora heard the bitterness in her brother's voice ring out like the sharpness of a knife.

She realised then that there was nothing more she could do to save herself.

She must do as he demanded or run away.

But, even as she thought about it, she knew how difficult it would be to leave without him being aware of it.

She had actually asked the Captain of the ship that had brought her from Edinburgh how often he put into Aulaypool and he had replied that he would be coming back in a week's time.

'I can hardly walk out without being caught and brought back,' Vanora thought.

As if Ewen knew what she was thinking, he said,

"Cheer up, Vanora, you are quite intelligent enough to do this for me without hurting yourself or anyone else. After all you are a McKyle and you don't enjoy knowing that the MacFiles are laughing at us and our discomfort?"

His voice sharpened as he added,

"They are very well aware that we are still suffering from the battle that we fought and lost so many years ago."

"Does it really affect the Clan?" she asked.

"Of course it does. You know them as well as I do. They want to hold their heads high and they want to be, if not superior to, then at least the equal of every other Clan in Scotland."

He threw up his hands as he declared,

"But here on their doorstep are their conquerors and I cannot imagine that any McKyle sees a MacFile without feeling embarrassed and humiliated by him.

There was nothing more Vanora could say. She knew that it was what her brother believed, even though it all seemed a little far-fetched.

But then how could they forget what had happened when Killdona Castle was only a few miles away?

She gave a deep sigh.

"Very well, Ewen," she said. "I will do what you want me to do. But I can only pray with all my heart that it will not make matters worse than they are already."

She knew by the expression on her brother's face that he was delighted he had won the battle between them.

Feeling she could bear it no more, she went from the room and up stairs to the bedroom she had always slept in.

Her luggage had already been carried up by one of the servants and there was a maid whom she recognised, who had looked after her in the past.

"It is Bessie!" she exclaimed.

"And it be yourself, Miss Vanora," Bessie cried.

She put her arms round the old woman and kissed her. She had been like a nurse to her after her old Nanny had left and had looked after her mother before she died.

"It be real nice to see you back here, Miss Vanora," Bessie said. "You've been away far too long and we've all missed you."

"And I have missed you, but I have enjoyed being in London and Uncle Angus has been very kind to me."

"So he should be," Bessie said, "and very pretty you be lookin' now you be dressed up and a young lady."

Vanora laughed.

"Is that what I seem to you? At the moment I feel very young, very helpless and, if you want the truth Bessie, rather foolish."

"Now what's been upsettin' you?" Bessie asked. "To be sure the Laird can make us all angry at times, but we listen to him just as we listened to your father."

"Is Ewen successful as a Chieftain?"Vanora asked.

She knew it was a question she could ask Bessie without being indiscreet, as dear Bessie had always been one of the family and nothing she said to her would go any further.

"It be like this, Miss Vanora," Bessie said. "Your father bullied them and expected whatever he wanted the moment he asked it and your brother be much the same. He were always a difficult child, as your mother would tell you, but he has his soft spots. They be hard to find, so us has to take him as he be, so to speak."

Vanora smiled.

"That sounds so like you, Bessie. It's worth coming back home just to hear you making me see things as they are and not as I want them to be."

"Now lookin' as you do," Bessie said, "you ought to have everythin' your own way. If a pretty woman can't have 'em, then who can?"

Bessie had always had something different to say to what anyone expected and her mother had loved her just as she loved her.

She gave the old woman a hug and said,

"I am going down to the river. I feel a little upset at present and I know that, if I walk beside it, it will soothe me as it always did. I almost feel it is alive and listens to what I have to say."

"You can be certain of that, Miss Vanora, so you go down and tell it your troubles. They'll sink to the bottom just like a stone and you'll soon forget 'em."

She ran downstairs and through the front door.

As she passed through the garden, she knew that it was not as well tended or as full of flowers as it had been when her mother was alive.

'I suppose,' she reflected, 'I ought really to come home and look after Ewen as he has no wife and make things as they always used to be.'

Then she realised that it was no use making plans until she had been to the interview that Ewen had arranged for her.

She felt herself shiver at the thought of it.

She could not really pretend to be someone she was not and, if she found the Stone, what would happen if she was caught carrying it out into the garden or even being concerned with it in any way?

She reached the river and stood looking at the water moving slowly towards the sea.

A salmon rose a little to the left of her and then it splashed and disappeared behind a stone.

It was all so familiar and so lovely and she felt as if a healing hand was placed on her forehead.

It took away her worries and the questions she kept asking herself.

It was almost as if the beauty of the river told her that everything would be all right.

She must trust in God and let things happen without trying to prevent them from doing so.

She walked along the river for a long time and then she realised that the sun was now sinking behind the hills and there was a faint mist coming up from the sea.

She went back slowly and by the time she reached the castle the sun had gone, yet the sky was still clear.

She looked up and thought that she saw the first twinkle of an evening star.

It was a sign, she told herself, of good luck and that was something she would surely need in the future.

'Help me, please help me, God,' she prayed.

She watched the river flowing away from her and saw the shadows deepen.

She had the strangest feeling that she was moving, not into something which was wrong and frightening but into a Fairyland.

The gates were just opening for her and she could not understand it, but the feeling was there.

This was something new.

Although it seemed to her totally impossible, she knew that she need not be afraid.

CHAPTER TWO

Neil MacFile, the Viscount File, had been pursued by women ever since he had left school.

He was the heir to one of the oldest Earldoms in Scotland and he was exceedingly rich.

He was very handsome and extremely intelligent.

His reports from the school that he had attended in Edinburgh were so complimentary that his father would query them.

He received a first class degree with honours at Oxford University without any difficulty.

And it was inevitable that he should find the Social world that surrounded the Prince Regent, soon to become King George IV, amusing and fascinating.

He was warned by all his contemporaries to have nothing to do with *debutantes*. They pointed out to him that he was a most marriageable catch and that ambitious mothers would have him at the top of their list.

There were, however, as he had heard whispered in London, a good number of lovely and exotic married ladies who enjoyed the company of young men like himself more than that of their busy or dull husbands.

He found this to be all too true.

He had enjoyed some delicious *affaires-de-coeur* with famous beauties whose husbands were either too busy in Parliament or preferred the 'Sport of Kings' which kept them in the countryside.

The Viscount was only too well aware of his duty to his Clan in Scotland and he had ideas of how he could improve his heritage once it came into his hands.

For the present time his father was very much in command and, although he consulted his son, he rejected ideas that were unusual or had not been tested in the past.

Because life was going so smoothly for Neil, it was inevitable that sooner or later he would become a little disillusioned.

He had been captivated by a very attractive beauty, who was only too willing to fall into his arms when he held them out.

She was lovely in an unusual manner with dark hair and huge eyes with a soft touch of green in them and she sported, he thought, the most perfect body that any woman could hope to have.

Lady Seymour had an attractive house in Mayfair and it was so easy for Neil to visit her late at night when returning from a Regimental dinner or some bachelor party given by his friends.

He began to think that he was really falling in love with her because Sybil seemed so helpless in many ways.

It appealed to him to have a woman ask his advice on every possible matter and she looked on him as if he was superior not only in strength but in intellect.

"How can you be so clever, darling?" she asked. "I love listening to you and you are so kind to help me with all my difficulties."

These difficulties of hers consisted mainly of lack of money and she confided in him that her husband had left her very little when he died.

She was therefore living on her capital, which she realised would eventually end in disaster.

She did not ask for money, but the Viscount was very generous. When he saw her bills at the end of the month, he paid them because he could well afford to do so.

Naturally he gave her the usual presents that every woman expects – flowers, scent and a number of jewels. These thrilled her so much he felt that he had been more generous than he actually was.

He began to think as time passed and he spent all the time that he could with Sybil when he was not in the Officers' Mess or on the Parade Ground that he was falling in love with her.

He did not ask why it was so different from what he had felt before, except that because she was so helpless he felt that he must protect her.

The bills seemed to increase, but it was of no great significance and he genuinely wanted her to be happy.

Then one afternoon he was leaving early, as the Colonel had asked him to dinner and he could not refuse.

The maid who showed him to the door said when he tipped her as he usually did,

"This'll be the last time you'll be a-seein' me, my Lord."

The Viscount, who was about to cross the pavement to step into his phaeton, stopped.

"You are leaving, Emily?" he enquired.

"Yes, my Lord. I just can't stand no more of 'er Ladyship's temper and the 'arsh things she says to me."

The Viscount was astonished.

He thought Emily an excellent servant and he could not believe that Sybil could be guilty of either of Emily's accusations.

"Now what has upset you?" he asked. "I am sure that your Mistress does not wish to lose you."

"I've stood all I can," Emily replied, "and I can't take no more. Screamin' and yellin' at me this mornin' she was, as if I were some guttersnipe! Hurtin' me with 'er 'airbrush 'cos I forgot with all I 'as to do to order the wine she offers your Lordship which you pays for."

The Viscount drew in his breath.

He could not believe what he was hearing and, as it seemed so incredible, he thought that he should persuade Emily to change her mind and stay with her Mistress.

He was aware that she was the only servant living in the house, which was a very small one.

When he dined there alone with Sybil, he invariably brought with him some delicacy such as *pâté de foie gras* or caviar.

"Now listen to me, Emily," he said in a conciliatory voice, "I am quite certain that, if Lady Seymour has upset you, it is just a mistake and she would be very sorry if she lost you."

"Don't you believe it, my Lord, she don't care for anyone but 'erself and never 'as. You've always been a gentleman to me and I thinks you should know the truth."

She fumbled in the pocket of her apron and brought out a crumpled letter.

"Just read this, my Lord, and you'll understand that what I've been a-tellin' you be the truth and not a lie. You're too trustin', that's what you be."

She pressed the piece of paper into his hand.

Then, as he added two more guineas to the two he had already given her, she dropped him a curtsey.

"God Bless you, my Lord," she said, "and I prays that one day you'll find a woman who be worthy of you."

She stepped and then the Viscount heard the door close behind him.

She had just been acclaimed by the King as one of the most beautiful women that he had ever seen and the Viscount had to admit that he thought the same.

The Countess Walton was indeed extremely lovely and the exact opposite to Sybil. She had fair hair and blue eyes and was a perfect English beauty with just a little extra that made her somehow unique.

It seemed surprising to the Viscount that he had not met her before and then he learned that she had been in mourning for her husband who had died in an accident.

She had stayed in the country where she had a large and comfortable house and her friends told her that she was wasting her looks and that London was waiting for her.

She had therefore obeyed them and instantly caught the attention of the King.

His Majesty gave party after party for her and the Viscount was present at one which in the usual lavish way of the King's entertaining was a very large one.

On his first sight of the Countess he knew that she eclipsed the beauty of every woman he had met.

He would not rest until he possessed her.

They danced together and he felt her body moving against his and there was an expression in her eyes that he was very familiar with.

He knew that it was just a question of time.

"How could you be so beautiful, my darling?" he asked later when she was lying in his arms.

"I think I must have kept it for you," she cooed.

Although he had heard all that before, the Viscount wanted to believe it.

Doreen, for that was her name, had made it quite clear from the first moment they met that he interested her more than anyone else.

It was only a few days before they became lovers and the Viscount had to admit that he had never known a woman who was so insatiable.

She looked like an angel and behaved like a tigress and, because he was so infatuated, he spent every moment he could with her.

The Countess had rented a house in Park Lane and the Earl learned that her husband had been a very rich man, and she herself had some money inherited from her father.

Her family lived in Northumberland and she was reluctant to come to London after she had been widowed.

As she told the Viscount,

"I must have been waiting until you, dearest, were here and it was Fate we should meet and love each other."

He found it decidedly sad that she had had such a short married life.

She had been only just twenty, when her husband, driving his phaeton far too fast, had collided with another vehicle in a very narrow lane. He had been killed instantly and it was only by a miracle that she had been spared.

"I was laid up for what seemed a long time," she said. "Then I had no wish to go to parties or even to meet other men."

"And now you have met me," the Viscount said.

"What could be more wonderful or more perfect?" Doreen asked.

Because she was so insistent, he found it difficult to concentrate on his Regimental duties.

All he could think of was Doreen holding out her arms as he arrived at her house in Park Lane and the large scented bed they always found themselves in immediately the candlelit dinner was over.

"I love you, I love you," Doreen said again and again. "Tell me, my wonderful handsome lover, that I hold your whole heart."

The Viscount, who had always been very much the King of his own castle, felt at times that he was being manipulated.

It was Doreen who had taken control, not himself.

He had very often been the hunted rather than the huntsman and yet once a love affair started he expected to be in control.

It passed through his mind several times that maybe Doreen was becoming too possessive and he would have to exert himself if he was not to let her take control of him.

She must, he thought, allow him to do the running and give the orders.

Then one night when they were both exhausted by the fire and excitement of their lovemaking, the Viscount was just thinking that it was time for him to return home.

Because he was always so late with Doreen, he did not keep his carriage waiting, but walked back from Park Lane to Berkeley Square.

It did not take him long, but at the same time when he was sleepy it was somewhat of an effort.

He was thinking that he should make a move, as otherwise it would soon be dawn and he had a great deal to do that morning.

Then in the soft coaxing voice he loved because it was so musical, Doreen said,

"If we are going to have children, which I know is important to you, Neil darling, I think that we should get married."

For a moment the Viscount was too astonished to move or breathe.

Then he was alert and, because it was something he had never thought of before, he closed his eyes.

When Doreen, whose face had been close against his neck, looked up, she saw that he was asleep.

Some minutes later the Viscount, with an extremely imaginative piece of acting, said,

"I must have fallen asleep. Why did you not wake me? You know I have to be up early in the morning."

"You have not been asleep long," Doreen replied.

"You have tired me out," he muttered with a smile.

He climbed out of bed and started to dress.

She lay watching him and to his relief she did not repeat what she had said before.

When he kissed her goodnight, she clung to him.

"I will see you tomorrow night," she sighed, "but it will seem a long time before I do."

"I will not be late," he replied, "and thank you, my lovely one, for a very wonderful evening."

He moved towards the door.

"Go to sleep at once," he said. "I want you to look beautiful tomorrow."

He did not wait for an answer. He ran down the stairs and let himself out of the front door.

As he closed it behind him, he was thinking with some alarm about what she had said.

It was almost as if she had thrown a bomb in front of him.

He had promised himself when he had first come to London that he would not marry until he was much older and then only because he must have a son, or for safety two or three sons, to carry on the Earldom.

It had never struck him for one moment that anyone like Sybil or Doreen would want marriage.

He loved them, but they were in fact only partners in an *affaire-de-coeur*.

That was very different in his mind to being tied for life to a woman who would bear his name and his children.

She must be pure and innocent when he married her.

Perhaps this idea had come to him from one of his ancestors and he must have been very much more moral than was expected today at the Court of King George IV.

Everyone knew of His Majesty's love affairs and they were talked about quite openly. His marriage had been a failure and his wife was behaving very badly, but fortunately in foreign countries rather than in England.

It was to be expected that as a man he would have other women in his life and he certainly made no secret about it and the Officers who served him did the same.

The Viscount as a matter of course had accepted the favours which were offered him so willingly and he put the idea of marriage completely aside until, he told himself, he became the Earl of Glenfile.

He would then be expected to spend much of his time in Scotland with his Clan and it was not until then that the question of marriage would arise.

He would then doubtless find someone suitable and acceptable to the Clansmen and it would be wise for her to be a Scot.

Now, he thought, Doreen had set him a problem he had not anticipated and it was definitely a difficult one.

He loved her, of course he did.

She was undoubtedly the most enticing woman that he had ever known, but he could not see her fitting in with those who would follow him as their Chieftain.

They would undoubtedly be shocked if they knew how he had behaved in England and it was very different from how he would conduct himself in Scotland.

Yet Doreen wanted to marry him.

As she was so beautiful and he was good-looking, their children would be outstanding.

It was a problem he had never imagined he would have to face for a long time.

Now he was involved and would have to make up his mind one way or the other.

It would be difficult to say to Doreen that he loved her, but did not consider her suitable to be his wife.

It might be even more difficult to marry her and try to make her behave in a way that would please the Clan.

It was no use thinking that the Clan did not matter simply because he was a long way from it. Their needs, their homage and they themselves were in his very blood.

Because his father was still the Chieftain, he need not apply himself for the moment to what was happening at The Castle.

Yet he knew that as soon as he took his father's place, the Clan would be all-important, as it had been to every Chieftain in the past all down the centuries.

Doreen was beautiful, more beautiful than anyone he had ever seen before.

Yet somehow he could not see her with the women of the MacFiles, listening to all their troubles, helping them with their children, worrying if there was a bad harvest or if there were too few fish to catch in the river.

How could he say that to Doreen without hurting her?

Although he had evaded the question tonight, it was one she would undoubtedly ask again very soon.

It preyed on his mind and he found himself not paying proper attention at the meeting he had that morning at the War Office.

It was only when it was over he realised that there were points he should have made but had not done so.

Back at the Barracks the Colonel sent for him and again he found it hard to concentrate.

It was with a sense of relief that he drove early in the evening to White's Club and he thought that, if he sat there quietly, he could think more clearly as he wanted to have something ready to say to Doreen.

She might easily approach him in the same way this evening as she had last night.

It was a relief to find that the coffee room was not full and he could sit quietly in a corner.

He ordered a drink from the Steward and then he sat back in his comfortable leather chair.

Yet he was hearing once again that soft seductive little voice saying,

"*If we are going to have children, I think that we should get married.*"

"What can I do? What the devil can I do?" the Viscount asked himself.

Then at that moment a voice said,

"Hello, Neil. I rather expected to see you here."

It was a man called Richard Dickenson, who had been at Oxford with him where they had been great friends.

So the Viscount replied in all sincerity,

"It's delightful to see you, Richard. I did not know you were in London."

"I have only come up here for a few days," Richard Dickenson said. "I was going to get in touch with you after

I had finished the long boring meetings I have had to have with my father's Solicitors."

The Viscount looked surprised, but he did not ask the obvious question.

"My father died a month ago," Richard Dickenson explained. "And, as you can well imagine, everything is a mess, although it's difficult to see the reason for it."

"I know just what you mean," the Viscount replied. "Solicitors always make the worst of everything simply to tell you at the end how clever they have been."

His friend laughed and sat down beside him.

"Let me stand you a drink," he said. "Surprisingly, I can afford it much better than I expected."

"I think under the circumstances you should have one with me," the Viscount said, "but we will not quarrel about it."

Richard Dickenson laughed, hailed a Steward and ordered champagne.

"I have been hearing about you, Neil," he said.

"Nothing to my advantage, I suppose."

"On the contrary. I hear that you are with the most acclaimed beauty in London and what man could ask for more?"

The Viscount laughed.

"What indeed? You must meet her, she is indeed very beautiful."

"I remember seeing her several years ago," Richard Dickenson said, "and I have heard of her since, because my mother knew her mother. I think that they were distantly related."

"That is interesting, Richard, you must certainly meet Doreen again now you are in London."

"I would love to. I have always been so terribly sorry for her that she had that dreadful accident with her husband so soon after they were married."

"It was certainly a tragedy for him," the Viscount said. "But Doreen has recovered from it now."

He thought as he spoke that she had not really been regretting the loss of her husband this past month.

"It was very bad luck for him," Richard Dickenson agreed, "and for her. After all no woman likes to think she can never have a child."

The Viscount stiffened.

For a moment he could not believe what he had heard.

And there was no possibility that Richard was not telling the truth.

It was impossible, totally and utterly impossible and, for him, as the only son of his father, to marry anyone who could not carry on the line.

He did not go back to Berkeley Square to change for dinner that evening. He dined at White's with Richard Dickenson.

*

The next morning a message came from Scotland asking him to come home immediately.

His father had had a stroke and the doctors thought it unlikely that he would recover.

The Viscount did not say goodbye to Doreen.

Nor did he write to her and let her know that he was leaving London. He felt that she would understand why he had gone when she read the newspapers.

He could not bring himself to speak to her.

She had deliberately tried to trap him and that was something he could never forgive.

37

She loved him in her own way that he admitted.

At the same time if he married her as she suggested, it would be a disaster.

How could she ever account for the fact that she could not provide him with an heir?

It would have been an utterly hopeless position to which there was no solution.

*

The Viscount travelled to Scotland as quickly as he possibly could.

As he did so, he could only think that he had had an amazingly narrow escape, or rather two escapes, from two unscrupulous women.

It made him feel frustrated and bitter.

He told himself firmly that never again would he be deceived.

As he was still quite young, the thorny question of marriage was not urgent.

Perhaps in ten years' time he would then consider it important that he have a son, an heir to follow him when he could no longer be Chieftain of the Clan.

But there was no hurry.

For the moment because he had been hurt, he felt that he disliked all women and had no wish for any woman to be in his life.

For amusement there were always the *courtesans* and they at least were frank and open about themselves and not interested in trapping a man, only in wheedling money out of him which was their profession.

What he loathed and what he would never forgive was that Sybil had merely wanted his money.

He had believed that she loved him for himself and then Doreen had been prepared to lie her way to the altar and make him in consequence suffer as only a Scot would understand.

And then he would not be able to give his people who believed in him and trusted him, a future they could be proud of.

'I have learned my lessons,' he thought bitterly.

The yacht, which had been sent for him, moved into the bay opposite Killdona Castle.

As it did so, he thought how beautiful it all looked in the afternoon sunshine and the light on the moors behind The Castle was exactly as he remembered it.

The towers were pointing high above the garden and he could see the profusion of flowers which were there to greet him.

As the yacht drew nearer, a number of people came running down the steps from The Castle and he knew that they had been waiting for him.

He felt his heart leap because he was sure of one thing and that was their loyalty and their faith in him and his family.

'That is what matters,' he told himself. 'Now I am in the North where I belong and I can forget the South with all its conspiracies and despicable deceptions.'

As the yacht drew nearer still, he heard the pipes beginning to play the tune he had known ever since he was a child.

It was *The Battle Song of the MacFiles.*

As he saw how many people were waiting for him, he was glad that he had put on his kilt and his sporran just in time.

He had actually not thought about it until the last moment and then he remembered that the whole staff of The Castle would be waiting for his arrival.

Some might be at the windows, but he was quite sure that the more enterprising would be up on the roof of the towers watching the sea with a telescope and this was the sort of attention that always touched him.

However much he might have enjoyed himself in London, there was nothing like coming home.

The yacht came to a standstill and he saw that the men waiting for him were each wearing a black band round his arm.

Then, as the anchor went down, the pipers played another tune that he also recognised.

It was *The Welcome to the Chieftain* and that told him without words that his father was dead.

CHAPTER THREE

The ninth Earl of Glenfile was buried in the family vault with honour and his Clansmen walked solemnly behind him.

The Service was very sincere and emotional and, as was usual in Scotland, only the men attended and went on afterwards to the wake.

There a huge amount of whisky was drunk and the new Earl and Chieftain made a speech.

He was genuinely very moved by the sorrow shown by the Clan on his father's death.

*

The next few days the new Earl spent talking with the Elders about the affairs of the Clan, because he was determined to alter a great number of customs he thought were old-fashioned and out of date.

Then the moment came when he was to receive the allegiance of all the Clansmen and take his father's place as Chieftain.

With the pipers standing on each side of him, he sat in the chair made of stag's horns that had been the throne of the Chieftain for two hundred years.

Nothing could have been more impressive.

Proudly dressed in their best kilts with plaids over their shoulders, the Clansmen came up one by one. They knelt in front of the new Earl and pledged their allegiance.

After which venison was cooked over fires in the grounds and the men and women of the Clan celebrated the opening of a new era.

They were delighted with their new Chieftain.

The Earl had known many of those present since he had been a small boy and he went round shaking hands with everyone.

He gave the impression that he would care for their well-being even better than his father had done and what was more he would make the Clan even more important than it had been in the past.

The festivities continued for several days and then the relations, who had come from various parts of Scotland to be present, left.

The Earl found himself alone with his aunt, Lady Sophie MacFile. She was his father's eldest sister and had never married, but she had devoted herself to helping poor Scottish families in the North.

She was the most charming and gentle woman and he had been very pleased to see her at his father's funeral.

"You must tell me, Neil," she said now, "when you want me to leave."

"The answer to that question is simple," he replied. "Never, unless you have something more pressing to do."

Lady Sophie looked at him in surprise.

"Do you mean it?"

"Of course I mean it. I shall be very lonely here in The Castle all by myself and it would be delightful to have you with me."

"But surely, my dear boy, you will be wanting your friends from the Regiment and others from London to stay with you, especially in the sporting season."

"I will think about that," the Earl replied. "At the same time I shall be in need of a companion and who could perform that function better than you?"

Lady Sophie laughed.

"You flatter me, but I would like to stay with you and to become more intimate with the women of the Clan than your father allowed me to be."

"Did he stop you from being friendly with them?" the Earl enquired in surprise.

"You must remember that your father thought that nothing which concerned the Clan was in any way perfect unless he did it himself. He did not trust anyone else."

The Earl grinned.

"That is true. I am sure that there are a great many things that have been left undone and I should be grateful if you would notify me of them."

"I will do that and I am very proud of you, Neil. I thought when I was watching you receive the homage of your people that you looked like a King."

"Now you are flattering *me*. But, of course, that is what the Chieftain of a Clan always feels. I think they regret the day when they had the power of life and death!"

He thought while he was talking to his aunt that he must learn more about the Clan than he knew already.

He was rather vague, he told himself, on the history of Scotland as a whole and, although he had been at school in Edinburgh, he was sure that there were many facts he had not learned or had forgotten.

They might be of assistance to him now and it was because he was thinking of this that he went to the library.

He was appalled at what he found there.

His father had never been a great reader, but even as a boy Neil had explored the library for history books.

He had read even when he was very busy with his Regiment or in London when he had the time and he was well aware that some of the books in the library of The Castle were of great value.

There were many first editions and some of them were very old and there had also been, he remembered, one part of a wall reserved for books on Scotland.

But over the years, while he had been away, people had pulled out books and, when they were finished with them, they put them back anywhere on the shelves.

There were at least three thousand books in the very large library and he knew that he could not find the time to put them all in order himself.

'I shall have to find a librarian,' he decided.

He sent for Mr. Tyler, the secretary to his father, who had been at The Castle for the last fifteen years.

"I am appalled at the state of the library, Tyler," he began when the secretary appeared.

"I was afraid you might be, my Lord," Mr. Tyler replied.

He was a small, very Scottish-looking man, who might, the Earl thought, easily have been an ancient Pict.

They had been small dark men until they had been overwhelmed by the Scots and Vikings and they had grown much taller when their blood was mixed. The Tyler family, however, he felt, must have remained undiluted for many generations!

Once again the Earl was thinking that he should learn more about the Picts and the Scots and what they had meant to Scotland itself.

"What I suggest we should do, my Lord," Mr. Tyler was saying, "is to advertise for a librarian."

"A good idea!" the Earl replied. "It will certainly keep him busy for at least a year."

When he left the library, the Earl carried with him a book on Scotland that had been written by a Scotsman only ten years ago.

He thought with a somewhat wry smile that quite a number of books had been published since and, of course, as his father was not interested, none had been purchased for the library.

The Earl was, however, not at all pleased when, a week later, Mr. Tyler informed him that the only applicant who had answered his advertisement was a woman.

"It would be much better to have a man," the Earl replied sharply.

"I am afraid, my Lord, that we are so far in the North that there are not too many unemployed intellectuals here. But if you wish, I can advertise the post in one of the Southern newspapers and see if there's any response."

The Earl considered for a moment and then he said,

"It might be best to see this young woman, who can start tidying things up until we find someone better."

"She has one very good reference, my Lord," Mr. Tyler said, "having been working for Lord Blairmond, who speaks of her very highly."

"I have, of course, heard of Lord Blairmond," the Earl said, "and I understand that he has now retired, except when he attends the House of Lords."

"He says in his reference," Mr. Tyler replied, "that he had not only found Miss Bruce exceptionally intelligent when dealing with his library but she had also helped him with a book he is writing."

"Well I shall not be writing a book at the moment," the Earl smiled.

"I have heard about some of the changes you have already brought in, my Lord," Mr. Tyler said, "and I do congratulate you because they are long overdue and will be of great benefit to the Clan."

"That is what I thought myself," the Earl replied with a note of satisfaction.

He then forgot that he had told Mr. Tyler to make an appointment for him to see this woman.

It was therefore quite a surprise when he told him that she was arriving for the interview that afternoon.

'I can expect,' he thought, 'that she will be middle-aged, ponderous and certainly over-talkative. I must make it clear from the very beginning that I do *not* have the time to listen to her.'

He left The Castle and only returned for a very late luncheon.

He apologised to Lady Sophie and told her that she should not have waited for him.

"I was not hungry, dear boy," his aunt replied. "I much preferred to wait and talk to you. I know you have been seeing to improvements on the river, which I thought for some time were long overdue."

"You are quite right," the Earl said. "I was rather surprised that my father did not do any more to the river. What I have done now will be a great help, I hope, to the fishermen who fish in it."

"Which should include yourself. It surprises me, Neil, that you have not brought in a salmon before now."

"I simply have not had the time," he answered. "I assure you that the Elders are full of matters they want me to inspect and I have not had a day off to enjoy myself."

"That is something you should certainly take next week," Lady Sophie said. "I think it would be a good idea if you asked one of your friends to come and stay. There are many salmon in the river at the moment and you used to be such a good fisherman when you were a small boy."

"I hope I have not lost the knack. You are so right, Aunt Sophie, all work and no play is good for no one."

He was still talking to his aunt when the butler came into the room.

Donald informed his Lordship that Miss Bruce was now waiting for him in the Chieftain's Room.

*

When Vanora had been told by her brother that he had written to the Earl for her appointment calling her Miss Bruce, she had laughed.

"Why Bruce?" she asked him. "As far as I know, there has never been anyone of that name in our family."

"That is one reason why I chose it. Then I thought that no one was more of a hero to us that Robert the Bruce, so why not use his name? I believe in fact that we are distantly related to him."

"I am delighted to be in the Royal circle," Vanora replied. "I only hope that I remember not to refer to myself in an absent-minded moment as a McKyle."

"In which case you will no doubt be kicked out of the door," her brother retorted, "and I will never forgive you for losing the Stone."

Although he was talking lightly, Vanora knew that there was many a true word spoken in jest.

She was quite certain that, if she could not obtain the Stone, Ewen would bear a grudge against her for the rest of her life.

And that might be almost as bad as being exiled from the Clan.

She therefore set off for The Castle, not feeling at all confident but depressed.

She was sure that, if she did not get the position, her brother would blame her for it.

Although she had no wish to work for the Earl of Glenfile, she knew that she must make the best of it.

She could not help, however, feeling a little thrill of excitement when The Castle came into view.

She turned in at the imposing gates. On either side were two stone turrets where the lodge-keepers lived.

Ewen had dropped her some way from the gates as she must not be seen approaching The Castle in case she was recognised by one of the MacFiles.

She was glad that she had put on comfortable shoes to walk in.

The drive was far longer than she expected it to be, although she knew that The Castle was at the far end on the sea and she remembered vividly just how beautiful it had looked as she had sailed past it before reaching home.

It had hardly seemed real and now, when she saw it from the other side, she was again conscious that there was something deeply romantic about the towers silhouetted against the blue of the sky.

The long mullioned windows were shining in the sun against the white brick of The Castle walls.

Vanora knew from what she had seen from the ship that the garden was ablaze with flowers as it sloped down to the sea.

There was a portico over the front door and, when she climbed slowly up the steps, there was no need for her to knock or ring the bell.

The door was opened immediately by a footman.

There were two men in the hall both wearing kilts of the MacFile tartan.

Before either could speak, an older man appeared, who was obviously the butler.

"I thinks you be Miss Bruce," he said with a broad Scots accent. "We're expecting you and I am Donald."

"I hope that I am not late, Donald," Vanora replied. "But the drive is longer than I anticipated."

"A great number of people have said that, miss," he replied. "Will you no come this way?"

He went ahead up a broad wooden staircase which was decorated with stags' heads and when they reached the top there was a passage carpeted with the MacFile tartan.

They walked for quite some distance along it before Donald opened a door.

The moment Vanora entered she knew that it was the Chieftain's room. It was exactly as a book she had read about The Castle years ago had described it.

Portraits and stags' antlers decorated the walls and everywhere there was a riot of tartan and Vanora wished she had read the book again before coming to The Castle.

She had been only fifteen when she had read it and her father found her reading it and took it away and flung it into the fire.

"I will not have you learning anything about our enemies," he had growled angrily. "And I will not have the name of the MacFiles mentioned here in my home!"

Vanora thought at the time that he was overdoing his hatred of the Clan who had defeated him and it was time that everyone forgot it.

But she knew that no one else would agree with her and that her father's violent hatred of the MacFiles was part of his life.

They had defeated him and one day in the future by some miracle he intended to defeat them.

How it would be done or when, it was impossible for him to decide. He only knew that he was convinced it would happen and, when it did, he would triumph over the enemy who had triumphed over him.

"I'll tell his Lordship you are here, Miss Bruce," Donald was saying.

He left the room and closed the door.

Vanora, instead of sitting down on a chair, walked to the windows.

They were long and high and just as they made The Castle beautiful from the outside they enriched the room within.

Through the windows, which opened outwards, she could see into the garden below and now she had a much better view of the flowers than she had had from the ship.

She knew how carefully the gardens must be tended to cope with the snow and cold of the winter.

Now under a clear sky the flowers were vivid.

A large stone fountain stood in the centre of them and the sunshine was catching the water as it flew upwards, then fell down forming a thousand tiny rainbows into the shallow bowl below.

It was all so lovely and Vanora could not help but regret that she had never been allowed to come here before, as The Castle after all was not far from her own home.

She looked out at the sea, blue in the reflection of the sky as the Mediterranean, as she thought that she could hear the soft wash of the waves where the garden ended.

It would be impossible, she felt, to live in a place so beautiful and at the same time be filled with hatred.

The Scottish Clan feuds which had existed all down the centuries seemed absurd when one compared them with the beauty of Scotland itself.

If only her countrymen could look at the moors and the rivers, they would no longer carry so much hatred in their hearts.

Intent on her musings and gazing at the enchanting garden below her, she did not hear the door open.

Then it was a footstep which told her that the Earl had joined her.

She turned round.

If he was astonished by her appearance after what he had expected, she was surprised at his.

The MacFiles had not been spoken of in her home except with hatred and the very name seemed not only to set fire to the words that were spoken but to contort the face and the mouth of the speaker.

Vanora had indeed expected the Earl to be ugly and unprepossessing, perhaps a short stout man.

To her surprise the man standing in front of her was almost the replica of a Viking.

Well over six feet tall, he had fair hair and blue eyes and he was wearing his kilt and Chieftain's sporran.

He was magnificent and for the moment completely overwhelming.

Vanora could only stare at him and she was aware that he was also staring at her.

She had no idea how lovely she looked with the sun behind her.

She was quietly and unobtrusively dressed in a soft blue suit, which accentuated the translucence of her very fair skin and the touch of red in her hair.

Vanora had come to The Castle wearing a little hat which did little to disguise what was beneath it and, as her hair was thick and naturally curly, it outlined her small pointed face.

As she opened her eyes in surprise, they seemed to be enormous.

The Earl thought that he had never expected to find anyone so lovely in the Highlands.

There was a short and slightly awkward silence.

Then with what seemed almost an effort he walked forward and held out his hand.

"Good afternoon, Miss Bruce," he said, "it is very good of you to come here and see me."

When he said the name that her brother had given her, Vanora pulled herself together and remembered why she was here in this magic castle.

"It is kind of your Lordship to see me," she replied.

"Shall we sit down?" the Earl suggested.

He walked towards two chairs which were in front of the mantelpiece and above it was a huge portrait of his grandfather in full Highland regalia.

Vanora sat down opposite him.

She was thinking as she did so it was lucky that she had not exclaimed in surprise at his appearance.

How could she ever have guessed that the man her father loathed and detested would look as if he had stepped out of a picture book?

He was undoubtedly the most handsome man that she had ever encountered.

'It is the Highland dress that makes him seem so different,' she told herself.

Yet she knew that none of the men she had met at her uncle's house, and there had been quite a few, could compare with the Earl.

"I understand," he was saying, "that you have been the librarian to Lord Blairmond. I have met him once or twice and I admire him for the considerable success he was as Secretary of State for Scotland."

"He is an exceedingly clever and interesting man," Vanora said.

"Yet you are prepared to leave him. Why are you doing so?"

It was a question Vanora had not expected and she gave him the first answer that came instantly into her head.

"I am a Scot."

The Earl laughed.

"So the Fatherland has called you back and you could not refuse?"

Vanora smiled, but did not answer and he went on,

"I suppose I am in the same boat. I find it is only when one returns to Scotland that one realises how much one has missed it while away."

"That is true, my Lord, and I had nearly forgotten how beautiful it is."

She looked towards the window as she spoke and the Earl said,

"I do agree with you. When I saw my castle when I arrived a month ago, I found it hard to believe that it was real and would not vanish when I touched it."

"Like Fairy gold," Vanora said and then they both laughed.

"I think the first thing we should do," he proposed, "is that you should come and see the library. It frightened me because there is so much to be done and you may well feel the same."

He then rose, went to the door and opened it.

As Vanora passed him, he thought that the way she walked was very graceful.

They went along the passage and down a different staircase and then they walked through a door that seemed to be at the very end of the building.

It was then she realised that the library was a very lofty room, enabling there to be a centre block of books in the middle of the room.

The books covered the walls and reached up to a ceiling which was exquisitely painted.

It must have been done, Vanora thought, at least two hundred years ago and was very well preserved.

Because she was looking surprised and entranced by the extent and height of the library, the Earl, who was watching her, enquired,

"Do you feel that you are capable, Miss Bruce, of coping with anything so large and so unusual?"

"I am thinking first," Vanora replied, "that you are very lucky. I only wish that I could have been brought up with a library such as this, my Lord. It would have meant more to me than I can possibly say in words."

"Then, of course, you are welcome to use it now," the Earl said.

"How could I do anything else?" Vanora asked.

She walked forward as she spoke and saw a finely carved marble fireplace in the centre of one wall, which must have been added later.

Over it there was a painting which she was certain was by Holbein and there were no other pictures in the room because every available space was covered by books.

The sofas and armchairs were all upholstered in red leather and the carpet was a fine Persian, but Vanora could only look upon the row after row of books.

She could see even from a distance that the books were out of order on the shelves and the height and binding did not match those around them.

"It is a Herculean task," the Earl said behind her, "and quite beyond the strength of a woman."

"It is a challenge, my Lord, and I think if you refuse to employ me now I shall leave The Castle in tears."

"Then I could not be so unkind," he smiled, "and all I can say, Miss Bruce, is that, if you can make even a small improvement on the muddle it is in now, then I shall be very grateful."

"I shall hope to restore this library to what it was intended to be," Vanora replied. "Equally it could not be done overnight, except with the help of a magic wand."

"Is that what you possess?" the Earl enquired.

He thought as he spoke that she looked somehow ethereal. Not only very different from the sort of woman he had expected, but more like one of the immortals.

He could not explain to himself what he meant, but there was something about this young woman that seemed to fit in with The Castle itself.

He was watching her eyes as she was gazing at the books and he knew instinctively that she loved them – not for the money they could bring but for their contents.

He did not know quite why he knew this, except, as he told himself so often, it was the fey in him.

Vanora turned to walk to the other side of the books in the centre of the room and he thought that she almost flew over the carpet and her feet hardly seemed to touch it.

But now, as she looked up at the books that almost touched the ceiling, he could see her full face.

It was then that the Earl was aware that she might have stepped out of the glorious painting on the ceiling.

As Vanora thought, it was the work of an Italian artist.

It depicted Venus attended by several Goddesses lying on the seashore with an array of Cupids who peeped from under stones or flew with garlands over their heads.

He was not dreaming or exaggerating, the Earl now told himself firmly.

Yet there was most certainly a distinct resemblance between the Venus or Aphrodite, as the Greeks called her, and the pointed face of this beautiful young woman.

The sunshine streaming in through the windows of the library illuminated the gold in her hair.

He then looked up at the ceiling again to see if it was true of any of the other Goddesses.

Vanora moved back towards him and enthused,

"How can you be so lucky, my Lord, to own all these marvellous books? Of course you must try to bring them up to date, as I can see that many of your ancestors have contributed to the library, so you must do the same."

"I agree with you, Miss Bruce," the Earl said, "but how soon can you start on this marathon task?"

"I feel that I should be asking how soon you would want me, my Lord," Vanora replied.

The Earl made a gesture with his hands.

"At this very moment or tomorrow morning."

"I think that tomorrow would be more convenient," Vanora replied, "and I should have asked before, do you expect me to stay in The Castle?"

She thought as she spoke that it was something her brother had omitted to mention.

It would be difficult to do what Ewen wanted if she had to stay in the village and she could hardly arrive back at some cottage carrying the Stone under her arm.

Also there would be more of an excuse for her to be found wandering in the garden or in the woods if she was staying in The Castle itself.

"I thought that Mr. Tyler would have discussed that with you," he replied. "I shall, of course, be delighted to have you as a guest, even though I feel in some ways that we are imposing on you and asking too much."

"As I have already said, my Lord, it is a challenge that no one who loves books could refuse. I can only do my best and if I fail to make it as perfect as it should be, then I am sure you will find someone else to complete it."

"Now you are talking of leaving before you have even started," he complained, "and that frightens me. I am sure that you have been sent as a messenger from Olympus to put my books in order and I shall be very disappointed if you do not use your magical powers to make it exactly as it is meant to be."

Vanora put up her hands.

"Now you are frightening me! At the same time, as I have already said, I will certainly try. I envy you more than I can possibly say for having anything so marvellous and, I should add, so exciting."

The Earl smiled.

"Now that is decided," he said, "I think you must come and meet my aunt who is looking after me and who is kind enough not to leave me alone in The Castle."

He thought as he spoke it was a good thing that Lady Sophie was here.

If he engaged this beautiful creature and was alone in The Castle with her, the tongues of the gossips would begin to wag.

Seeing how lovely she was, he was certain that she must have been a success in London, even though she was working for someone as elderly as Lord Blairmond.

They walked up the stairs and, as they did so, the Earl was thinking that in her own way this Scots girl was as outstanding as Doreen had been and, if the King saw her, he would agree with him.

"And did you enjoy yourself in London," he asked aloud, "besides working for Lord Blairmond?"

"If you mean, did I go to many dances and balls?" Vanora replied, "the answer is 'no'. My mother died soon after I started work and by the time I was out of mourning there was so much to do that there was little time for what Lord Blairmond thought of as frivolities."

The Earl laughed.

"He did not want to waste any of his time, but he was wasting you on his books and papers."

"I did not think of it like that," Vanora said. "I enjoyed the work and I can assure you Lord Blairmond's autobiography will be a sensation when it is published."

"Then I would hope he gives honour where honour is due," the Earl said, "for I am sure a great deal of its success will be due to you, Miss Bruce."

Vanora smiled.

"That is very flattering, my Lord, but I doubt if any of it is true. However, it has at least given me a great deal of experience and that is what you require at the moment."

The Earl opened the door into the drawing room.

Lady Sophie was sitting by the tea-table, which had been arranged in front of one of the windows.

"Oh, here you are, Neil," she said. "It may seem rather soon after such a late luncheon, but I am sure that you will enjoy a cup of tea."

"But of course," the Earl said, "and I have brought Miss Bruce with me, who I am glad to say has promised to undertake the task of restoring the library."

Lady Sophie had turned round as they approached and, when she saw Vanora, her eyes widened for a moment in surprise.

Then she said quietly,

"That is good news. I am sure that we shall enjoy having Miss Bruce here and being able to find a book when we want one."

The Earl pulled a chair out from under the table for Vanora to sit on and then he sat down himself.

He ate nothing although he accepted a cup of tea.

Lady Sophie wanted to know where Vanora was staying and how long she had been in Scotland.

Vanora was afraid of making a mistake and so she answered the questions as briefly as possible.

She felt that Lady Sophie thought it strange that when she was so young and good-looking why should she want to do anything so difficult and to most people so dull as to become a librarian.

But Lady Sophie was a strong admirer of Lord Blairmond and, when she spoke about him, Vanora thought that he would have been pleased at hearing how much he was admired.

She was very aware of how beautiful the drawing room was and the pictures in it were certainly outstanding.

She recognised a Reynolds and a Gainsborough and she thought the one at the end of the room was a Raeburn.

She had listened all her life to her father's hatred of the Earl and The Castle and she had therefore expected that the MacFiles would not be particularly cultured. And they would certainly not have a liking for all that she admired.

It was her mother who had taught her about artists, paintings and fine furniture.

Mrs. McKyle had been proud of her relationship with the Duke of Buccleuch and she would tell her family whenever they encouraged her to do so about the treasures that were to be found at his castle.

She had been thrilled when King George IV had stayed there when he arrived in Edinburgh two years ago.

That the visit had been such a success had exceeded the hopes of the most optimistic politicians and it would, they believed, restore Scotland's faith in herself.

Some years earlier six thousand workers had gone on strike in Glasgow and three of their leaders had been executed and Vanora recalled how distressed her mother had been.

It had been a brilliant idea of George IV to go to Scotland and Sir Walter Scot had called all the Highland Clans to Edinburgh to honour the King.

Vanora remembered how much her mother longed to go to Edinburgh herself, but unfortunately she was not well enough.

Her father, who disliked the English intensely, had no intention of making such a long journey. Other Clans might go, but he did not even suggest it to his.

None of the McKyles were therefore lucky enough to enjoy the excitement, the parades and the fireworks with which the King was greeted.

As Vanora sat at tea talking to Lady Sophie, she wished her mother could have known anyone so charming.

In a way Lady Sophie was very much like her.

She had often told her daughter how she had fallen in love with her father the moment she had seen him and how he had felt the same about her. He had been young and handsome in those days and not eaten up with hatred of the MacFiles.

'Mama ought to have lived in a castle like this one,' Vanora thought and then she told herself that she must not be ungrateful.

Their own castle was not so grand and certainly not so majestic. It was, however, a home she could be proud of and where as a child she had been very happy.

It was such a pity, she thought, that her brother was carrying on the feud between the two Clans.

Although she had only just met the new Earl, she felt that he would disapprove of anything so out of date and unpleasant.

'Maybe,' she thought, 'I might ask him if he would give me the Stone willingly and without any more trouble about it.'

Then she told herself that she was being absurdly optimistic.

Even if the Earl wished to be so generous, he would meet a great deal of opposition from his Elders and there were in the Clan those who had suffered for many years at the hands of her own people.

She was quite certain that there were still Clansmen who deliberately preyed on the boundaries of each other's land, stealing a young foal, shooting each other's birds and, when it was possible, poaching in each other's rivers.

When she thought about it all, it seemed hopeless and with a sigh she knew it was no use thinking wistfully.

She had to do what Ewen had sent her here to do, however wrong it seemed to her.

CHAPTER FOUR

When Vanora returned home, Ewen was delighted that she had been accepted at The Castle.

"Now we can really get things going." he said. "As soon as you find the Stone, let me know and I will arrange for someone to be waiting at the edge of the wood to take it from you."

"How do you think I am going to get it there?" Vanora enquired.

"It is rather heavy," her brother conceded a little reluctantly. "It would be rather easier if you could push it in something."

"Really, Ewen," Vanora scolded him, "you might have thought this one out before! After all I can hardly suddenly produce a pram and say I have a child! And they will be surprised if I walk about pushing a wheelbarrow."

"You will have to use your brains," her brother said in a lofty tone. "I am sure that, once you find the Stone, you will be able to think of some way of spiriting it away from The Castle."

He did not wait for his sister to reply, but walked out of the room shutting the door behind him.

Vanora gave a little sigh.

It had always been the same with Ewen. He asked for the impossible and then expected people to treat it as if it was something completely natural.

She packed her clothes and then Ewen took her to his friends, the Rosses.

He had already confided in them that his sister had an appointment at The Castle with regard to work she had been doing in London and did not want the Earl to know who she was and that was why he was relying on them to take her there.

The Rosses were a pleasant quiet couple, although Vanora remembered that her mother had thought them to be rather boring.

They were obviously very impressed that she was going to The Castle, having never been there themselves and she could only hope that they would not talk to their neighbours afterwards.

Ewen had assured her that they were completely reliable and trustworthy. However, she thought that, when it came to gossip, it was difficult to trust anyone.

Vanora had decided that she would not arrive too early in the morning and it was therefore eleven o'clock when Mr. Ross dropped her at The Castle front door.

She thanked him profusely.

However, she knew that he was enjoying having a closer look at The Castle than he would have had before and was only wishing that he could go inside.

A footman came down the steps to collect the two cases she had brought with her.

Donald welcomed her warmly.

"It's nice to see you again, Miss Bruce," he said. "I hears you be joinin' us and puttin' the library to rights."

"I hope to do so," Vanora replied. "But, as you are aware, it's not going to be an easy task."

"It's better you than me, miss," Donald stated. "I haven't the time to read books and that's the truth."

Vanora thought that might apply to quite a number of people, who had no idea what they were missing.

She was shown by the housekeeper, whom she had not met before, to a comfortable room and to her delight it was at the back of The Castle and overlooked the sea.

"I was hoping to have a room with a view," she said, "but I was afraid I was asking too much."

"There be plenty of choice here at this moment," the housekeeper replied. "It's been very quiet since his late Lordship, God rest his soul, were so ill."

She paused for a moment before she added,

"We've all been hopin' his new Lordship'll have a party or two. It'd cheer things up and, as you can see, Miss Bruce, there be bags of room to accommodate 'em all."

Vanora found it took her some little time to walk from her bedroom to the library.

She went in to find that there was no one waiting for her and she had not expected that there would be.

She went first to the writing desk, which was at the far end in front of one of the windows.

She looked to see if there was paper, pens and she hoped a book that she could use to make a catalogue.

To her surprise she found that everything that she might need was there and she thought it must have been the Earl's secretary who had realised what she would require.

This was confirmed when Mr. Tyler came to visit her.

He shook her warmly by the hand and told her how pleased he was to see her.

"I don't mind telling you, Miss Bruce," he said in a confidential tone, "I was half afraid that the job of clearing up this mess would fall on me and I've a great deal to do without that."

"It is very kind of you to have left all the things I require ready for me," Vanora replied. "And, as I don't want to bother his Lordship, I hope you will not mind if I come to you with any questions."

"You come as much as you like," Mr. Tyler said. "You'll find my office just inside the front door. It's easier for me to have it there so that people can pop in and out without having to ring the bell or worry the staff."

Vanora thought that he was a pleasant little man, but she was quite certain that he would not know a great deal about books.

She sat at the desk and looked round her wondering where she should begin.

Finally she decided she would start on what looked the oldest and would therefore be the most valuable books.

She noticed that occasionally on the shelves there were books such as one could buy at the seaside or in a village shop.

They were not the type of literature that one would expect to find in such an impressive and unique library.

She started to work and soon found several books which she knew were of significance.

Then she found one that seemed older than the rest and, because it was in Gaelic, she had difficulty in reading the name on the very faded cover.

She stared at the book as if she could hardly believe what she was seeing and then, as her find was so exciting, she felt impulsively that she must tell the Earl.

Holding the book tightly in her hands she ran down the corridor on the ground floor directly to the front door.

Donald was there and she said to him,

"Is his Lordship at present in The Castle? I must speak to him about this book."

"His Lordship should be back at any minute," he replied. "Is something wrong, Miss Bruce?"

"There is nothing wrong, but very very right."

As she spoke she heard the sound of horse's hooves outside and, as one of the footmen hurried to open the front door, she saw the Earl dismounting.

He patted his horse on the back before handing it to a groom and then walked up the steps to the front door.

"I am not late, Donald?" he said to the butler.

"No, my Lord, you still have five minutes to spare," Donald replied, "and Miss Bruce wishes to see you."

The Earl was taking off his hat and riding gloves and he was then aware that Vanora was standing at the other end of the hall.

"Good morning, Miss Bruce," he said. "I am at your disposal if you don't make me late for luncheon, as I am feeling exceedingly hungry."

"I will only keep you a moment or so," Vanora replied, "but I had to show you the book I have just found."

The Earl looked surprised. He did not think that a book could be of any particular importance.

He started to walk up the stairs as Vanora said,

"I found it pushed at the very back of a shelf behind some other books, so it may have been there unnoticed for a very long time."

"And you think it is of significance," the Earl said, glancing at the book she carried it in her arms.

It was quite a large one and she was holding it with two hands as if it was very precious.

Because Vanora wanted to surprise him, she did not reply.

They entered the drawing room and the Earl walked towards the window as if he thought he must look at the book in the strongest possible light.

Then, because he could see how excited Vanora was, he asked,

"Now what is all this about and why are you so pleased at what you have discovered?"

Vanora held out the book towards him and, as he took it in his hands, she told him,

"It is a copy of '*Foirm na Nurrnuidheadh*,' and it is the first book ever printed in Gaelic in Scotland in 1567."

"Is that true?" the Earl exclaimed. "I had no idea that any book was printed so early or that I owned a copy."

"It was written by Bishop John Carswell," Vanora replied, "and I remember Lord Blairmond saying that he had seen a copy of it in the British Museum and wished that he possessed one himself."

The Earl turned the pages of the book slowly.

"It is certainly a triumph that we should have one," he said. "I shall make enquiries amongst the other Clans to see if we can make them envious."

"I thought you would be pleased, my Lord, and I think you are very lucky because it seems complete and has not lost any of its pages."

"It is certainly your first triumph, Miss Bruce," he said. "We must tell my aunt about it and it will certainly be a new topic of conversation for us over luncheon."

Vanora looked at him and, as he was perceptive, he asked her,

"What is worrying you?"

"Nothing," Vanora replied. "I was just wondering if I was expected to have luncheon with you. I always ate luncheon with my previous employer, but I understand that a librarian, like a Governess, takes her meals where she is working."

The Earl laughed.

"That may be correct in England, but I am sure in Scotland we are much more friendly. Tyler does not come in for luncheon because he has a cottage in the grounds and a wife waiting for him. But it would be very inhospitable, Miss Bruce, if I expected you to eat alone in the library."

"Then I am very grateful to accept your Lordship's invitation to come to the dining room," Vanora smiled.

"And that is where we must go now or my aunt will tick me off as she usually does for being late!"

They walked from the drawing room to the dining room and it was even more impressive that Vanora had expected.

It was a very large room and the long polished table was laid for three places at the far end of it.

As the Earl and Vanora entered, Lady Sophie came in through another door.

"I heard you were back, Neil," she began, "and I must congratulate you on being so punctual."

"I was just telling Miss Bruce that you would tick me off if I was late," the Earl said, "and I can assure you that I made my horse gallop faster than he has ever done to be here on time."

"The trouble with your horses," Lady Sophie said, "is that they did not have enough exercise when your father was so ill."

She paused for a moment to say,

"Good morning, Miss Bruce, I do hope you are not too exhausted by what you have found waiting for you in the library."

"It is what Miss Bruce has just found," the Earl exclaimed, "that we are going to tell you all about, Aunt Sophie, and I am sure that you will be very surprised."

Lady Sophie was both surprised and very delighted when Vanora told her what she had found.

"I expected you to say that you had found a *First Folio* of Shakespeare," she said. "I have always been told that there is one here, but I have never seen it."

"Is there really a *First Folio* of Shakespeare in the library?" Vanora asked towards the end of luncheon,

"I remember being shown it by one of my Tutors several years ago," the Earl answered. "But, of course, it might easily have disappeared since then."

Vanora gave a little cry of horror.

"Oh, I would hope not! Surely you should have something to protect what is in your library. If there are items in it like this book and a *First Folio* of Shakespeare, you might attract thieves who could then spirit them away without your even being aware that they had gone."

"I have often thought of that," the Earl said. "But my father believed that, as we have so many menservants in The Castle, they would keep the burglars away and there is always someone in the grounds who would be suspicious if they saw strangers."

Vanora thought that it was all rather casual, but it was not her business to proffer advice.

She enjoyed the excellent luncheon and, as some of the things she said made the Earl laugh, she hoped that he had not been too disappointed in having her as a guest.

However, she hurried back to the library.

She entered the ancient book in Gaelic in her new catalogue and then she began to search for the *First Folio* they had been talking about over luncheon.

She remembered hearing that it was entitled, '*Mr. William Shakespeare, Comedies, Histories and Tragedies*', but not the actual year it had been published in.

She turned over a great number of books which she thought would be of interest to any collector, but there was no sign of the *First Folio.*

However she did find a seventeenth century Gaelic document called '*Fernaig Ms*'. It had been compiled by Duncan Macrae of Inverinate in 1688 and contained lines of verse that were mostly political or religious in content.

She had a feeling that it would not interest the Earl greatly, although she was sure that it was very valuable.

She went on searching until Donald came to tell her that tea was now ready in the drawing room and that Lady Sophie was expecting her.

By this time Vanora's hands were dusty from the books and, when she went to wash, she saw how untidy her hair was.

She also thought that tomorrow she would borrow an apron from the housekeeper to cover her clothes.

The Earl did not come in to tea and so being alone with Lady Sophie made it inevitable that she was asked a great many personal questions.

Because these inevitably concerned herself, Vanora felt uncomfortable and she was afraid of making a mistake.

"I have known a great many Bruces," Lady Sophie said in her soft voice. "I wonder which particular branch you belong to."

"I think all the Bruces," Vanora managed to say, "are so proud of being descended from Robert, King of Scotland, that they have never concerned themselves with anything else."

Lady Sophie laughed.

"That is true and, of course, they are a very large Clan. So where is your family home situated?"

Vanora had to think quickly, realising that this was dangerous ground.

"When my father and mother were alive," she said, "we had a house on the West Coast. But since their death I have moved about a great deal and have been in London lately, as you already know, with Lord Blairmond."

"It must have been most interesting working for him," Lady Sophie said.

Vanora agreed and, by talking about her uncle, she managed to prevent being asked any more uncomfortable questions as to where the members of her family lived.

She walked slowly back to the library.

As she did so, she was thinking that Lady Sophie was so charming and the Earl so kind that it was wrong for her to be accepting their hospitality.

If Ewen wanted the Stone so badly, he should have stolen it back himself and it struck her that was what she might have to ask him to do.

The Stone might be attached to a wall or enclosed in a case that she could not move anyway and so far she had not seen any sign of anything that looked anything like the Stone.

There were ancient documents framed on the walls and a great number of historical relics like suits of armour and shields surrounded by claymores.

There was, however, nothing to be seen that looked as if it could contain the Stone.

'There is no hurry,' Vanora told herself when she was in the library. 'If I am seen in parts of The Castle which have nothing to do with books, it might make the servants suspicious.'

When the evening came, again she was wondering if she should dine with the Earl.

Donald answered this for her by coming into the library with some candles.

"Now don't go strainin' your eyes, Miss Bruce," he said. "I've brought you some candles. But it'll soon be time for you to be dressin' for dinner. His Lordship eats at eight o'clock and her Ladyship's waitin' in the drawing room at exactly five minutes to the hour."

She therefore tidied up her desk and went to her bedroom.

She had brought with her several pretty evening gowns she had worn in London. Two were more elaborate which she had worn to a ball or a Reception.

There were also some simpler but more attractive ones she had bought for dining alone with her uncle.

Actually he had so many people wanting to see him that seldom a week went by when there were not a number of visitors and he preferred to see them at dinnertime as then they did not interrupt his work on his book.

Tonight Vanora chose a gown of very pale green that resembled the leaves in spring.

It made her look, the Earl thought, like a nymph who might have risen from the sea.

Once again he found the touch of red in her hair alluring and it was very different from that of any other Scots woman he had ever seen.

Many of them were red-headed, but it was not a particularly pretty red.

He thought, as he had before, that Miss Bruce must have been a success in London, whatever she might say.

"I am sure," he said at dinner, "that you are going to be very bored up here in the Highlands without all the admirers you must have had in London."

"I can assure you," Vanora replied, "I was working very hard on Lord Blairmond's book and the people who came to the house admired him, not me."

"I don't believe a word of it," the Earl said, "but I am so delighted that you are finding the library absorbing. Otherwise I have the feeling that you might vanish into the fountain or into the sea where I am convinced you belong!"

Vanora laughed before she answered,

"That is something I certainly missed in London."

"Was your home in Scotland near the sea?" the Earl asked.

She realised that she had made a mistake and was back trying to avoid saying too much about herself.

When dinner was over, they went into the drawing room.

The Earl offered Lady Sophie and Vanora a liqueur and then poured himself out a brandy.

He was exceedingly elegant in his evening clothes and Vanora thought that no Scotsman could have looked more impressive.

He sat down in a chair next to Vanora and said,

"Now I want you to tell me why, at your age, which I am certain is very young, you are wasting your time on musty books and old men?"

Vanora laughed because she could not help it.

"You may think it a waste of time, my Lord," she parried, "but I think it is very good for my brain."

"Your brain will last very much longer than your looks," the Earl said, "so I think that you should be making the most of them if you have not already done so!"

She knew from the expression in his eyes that he was just as curious about her as Lady Sophie was.

She knew that she should be very careful and that she must not say anything to make them suspicious that she was not who she pretended to be.

Aloud she said,

"I find it very boring to talk about myself when I want to learn a deal more about this beautiful and exciting castle and, of course, if the Gods are kind, to find you some more special and valuable books, my Lord."

"I think that is asking too much, but then you have certainly got off to a good start. I am only wondering, as you have already suggested, if we are keeping our treasures as safely as they deserve."

"You have so many treasures," Vanora said looking at the pictures. "When I first entered the library, I was so excited at seeing the Holbein over the mantelpiece and, of course, you have many fine and exceptional pictures here."

She looked round as she spoke, most of the pictures were portraits and they were all, she was sure, by famous artists.

The Earl smiled.

"I know," he remarked, "that you are admiring the picture of my grandmother by Sir Joshua Reynolds."

"It is very beautiful, my Lord, but he always made his women look so lovely that I have often wondered if he flattered them or if they were really like that."

"If he was alive, I am sure that he would want to paint you," the Earl replied, "and I am just wondering who there is today who could do you justice."

Vanora laughed.

"That is something that is very unlikely to happen and would cost a great deal of money. It's a waste of time talking about it."

She paused for a moment and then went on,

"What I would like to do, if you will permit me, my Lord, is to walk all over The Castle seeing your treasures in every room and being, I may say, envious because you have so much."

The Earl made a gesture with his hands.

"They are all at your disposal. I am only hoping that, when you admire what I possess, you will also have an appreciative eye for the owner."

Vanora smiled.

"You know quite well that I am longing to say that you must have Viking blood in your veins, but I am too polite to do so."

"I am sure you are right, there are many stories told of the Vikings who came to this part of Scotland. There is actually a legend that a Viking King stayed in The Castle and fell in love with the Chieftain's daughter of the time."

"And what did the Chieftain have to say about it?"

"That is not related," the Earl answered. "But, of course, I and my forebears may well be the answer to what happened when he stayed here!"

"It's a very romantic story and I would like to think it is true," Vanora said.

She then hesitated before she asked,

"Has every member of your family looked like you, my Lord?"

"I have always been told that a number of them have. You will see as you tour The Castle that there is a delightful portrait of my grandfather who I have a close resemblance to."

"Perhaps there is a book about him, my Lord."

"There have been a few books about the Clan as a whole," the Earl replied, "but the history of the family has never been written."

Vanora clasped her hands together,

"Then that is something you must do, my Lord."

The Earl was silent for a moment and then he said,

"I will think about it. But if I do, I will have to ask you to help me."

"I expect you will find plenty of people willing to do that and, for the moment, as you are well aware, I shall be too busy working in the library."

She rose as she finished speaking and said,

"If you will forgive me, my Lord, I think I should go to bed. I am a little tired after all the excitement of the day and there is a great deal to do tomorrow."

"But of course," the Earl replied. "You are very sensible."

As he stood up, Vanora looked at Lady Sophie.

She had fallen asleep in her chair and presumably had not heard the conversation that had just taken place.

Perhaps, Vanora thought, that was a good thing, as Her Ladyship might easily have considered that she was being too familiar on such a brief acquaintance.

The Earl saw that his aunt was asleep at the same time as Vanora did.

His eyes twinkled and they both walked silently across the floor to the door.

He opened it and then, as Vanora passed through it, he followed her.

Outside he held out his hand and took hers.

"I would like to thank you, Miss Bruce," he said, "not only for what you have found today but for all your enthusiasm and interest. It is delightful for me to have you here and I am very grateful."

"I only hope I shall find more treasures tomorrow," Vanora managed to say.

He still had her hand in his.

As she felt the strength of his fingers, she thought how strong he was.

It was as much a part of him as his extraordinary good looks.

She was then aware that the Earl had not released her hand and he was looking down at her in a somewhat strange manner.

"I am just hoping," he said as if she had asked, "that you will be here tomorrow."

"Why should I not be, my Lord?"

"Because, as I have already said, the sea may be calling you or perhaps the wind from the moors will carry you up to the top of them and I will never see you again."

Vanora gave a little laugh.

At the same time her eyes flickered and she could not look at him.

"I think both are unlikely," she said, "and I will be here for breakfast and ready to go to work."

"If you promise me that is what you will do," the Earl said, "I shall not worry, otherwise I shall undoubtedly have a sleepless night."

Vanora laughed again.

"I think that is unlikely, my Lord."

She took her hand from his.

Then she walked away quickly down the corridor that led eventually to her room.

She had the feeling that, as she went, his eyes were following her and he had not gone back into the drawing room.

She did not look round.

When she reached her bedroom, she thought that he was very much more perceptive than she had imagined any man could be.

One day, and it might be any day, when she found the Stone, she would disappear.

But she would not be lost in the waves of the sea or in the winds of the moor.

She would merely go back to Ewen.

He only wanted the Stone because he hated and loathed the MacFiles, who had taken it from him.

Just to think about it spoilt the enchantment of The Castle.

She had felt all through dinner that she was taking part in a play and she did not like to think that she was deceiving the Earl and his charming aunt.

When she did leave, they would think of her very differently from what they were thinking of her now.

Such thoughts upset her and they broke the spell that she had been enveloped in ever since she had come to The Castle.

Vanora went to the window.

She pulled back the curtains and looked out.

There was a moon rising in the sky and the stars were reflected in the sea.

There was the scent of the flowers from the garden and a faint wind was moving the leaves in the trees just below her.

It was all so incredibly lovely, a picture that had an irrepressible enchantment for anyone who looked at it.

She felt that she was a part of it all.

The moonlight touched the water rising and falling into the fountain and turned it to silver. It was also making its way into her heart.

'This is all a Fairytale,' she told herself and she knew that it was something she could not express in words and yet she responded to it with every nerve in her body.

Then suddenly, as if it made her afraid, she moved from the window.

She pulled the curtains back into place.

When she finally climbed into bed, she lay awake for a long time.

She was trying to think clearly and sensibly about what she was doing, but she found it impossible.

*

The next morning Vanora was downstairs early in the library and she had catalogued quite a number of books before breakfast.

When she went into the breakfast room, she found herself alone.

Donald informed her that his Lordship had gone fishing and her Ladyship was breakfasting in her room.

Vanora therefore ate breakfast quickly and went back to the library.

The sunshine coming through the window made her long to go out into the garden, but she felt that she must do some work and perhaps snatch a little time off later.

She found several books of great interest, but once again the *First Folio* of Shakespeare eluded her.

She did, however, discover to her surprise that one of the Earl's relatives had left some of the novels of Sir Walter Scott in the library.

There was *Waverley* and *Guy Mannering* and also *The Antiquary*.

And it was Sir Walter Scott who had arranged the triumphant visit of the King to Scotland two years ago.

Vanora was sure that some of the Earl's relations must have gone to Edinburgh and perhaps they had hastily bought the books by Sir Walter Scott so that they would not appear ignorant of his fame when they met him.

She also considered it stupid of her father to have refused to allow the McKyle Clan to take part in all the celebrations.

'The trouble is,' she thought to herself, 'in Scotland we have far too many feuds starting with the English and continuing on amongst our own people.'

She now wondered if the Earl was strong enough or patriotic enough for a great task and that was to unite the North of Scotland with the South of whom they had often spoken scathingly.

And to make the whole country unite to promote new schemes of economic development and to improve the education of their people.

This would, of course, bring them more prosperity.

It was just a dream and yet she was thinking that someone like the Earl might be capable of doing it.

'Perhaps I can talk to him about it,' she reflected.

Then she remembered why she was in The Castle!

How could she steal from the Earl and at the same time want him to be of more influence than he was already.

There was no sign of him at luncheon time and she realised that he would have taken his luncheon with him when he went to the river.

Lady Sophie was very interested in what she had been doing in the morning and, when Vanora told her that she had found the novels of Sir Walter Scott, she said,

"I enjoyed reading him myself and I am always hoping that he will write some more books."

"Would you like me to bring you one of them from the library now?" Vanora asked her.

Lady Sophie shook her head.

"I find it tires my eyes to read for long," she said. "But, of course, I am very interested in everything you discover and it's so good for Neil to take an interest in The Castle."

Vanora looked surprised.

"Has he not done so in the past." she asked.

Lady Sophie shook her head.

"He has spent much more time in England than in Scotland and it was inevitable that he should be such a success in the Social world which means so much to His Majesty."

Vanora knew that this was quite understandable as, looking so handsome and so dashing, the Earl would have naturally been talked about in what was known as the *Beau Monde*.

"I have been so worried about him at times," Lady Sophie was saying, "because, of course, he should marry and have an heir. But the beautiful women with whom he enjoyed himself would not be the right sort of wife for the Chieftain of the MacFiles."

Vanora knew this to be true.

"I am sure there must be plenty of suitable young women in Scotland," she said, "as well as in London."

"They might be suitable," Lady Sophie said, "but if one is honest they are seldom beautiful. The women Neil spends his time with in London are acknowledged as the great beauties of the year."

She gave a sigh and then went on,

"To be honest, my dear, I was very frightened in case he married the last one he was attracted to."

81

"Was she very beautiful?" Vanora enquired.

"I believe the King said she was the most beautiful woman he had ever seen and everyone knows that he is a good judge."

She gave a little laugh and then she sighed again.

"One day, my dear, when you have sons of your own," she said, "you will worry, as we all do, over whom they will marry. With someone of such consequence as my nephew, it is vital that he chooses the right woman."

There was silence and then Lady Sophie added,

"I don't want my nephew to be bored in Scotland, so I have asked some young people to stay and they will be arriving tomorrow."

After she had spoken, there was a short silence and then Vanora said,

"I am sure if you have done that, ma'am, it would be a mistake for me to have my meals in the dining room. I shall quite understand if I can have them elsewhere."

Lady Sophie smiled.

"That is very sensible of you and, of course, as you say, it would be correct. I will therefore arrange with the housekeeper that you use one of the boudoirs as a sitting room. I think there is one almost next to your bedroom."

"That would be very convenient," Vanora replied.

At the same time her heart sank.

She knew that it was ridiculous of her, yet she was disappointed that she would not be able to continue talking to the Earl.

As she went back to the library, she said to herself,

'You are being quite ridiculous. You are not here to enjoy yourself, but to do exactly what your brother as Chief of the Clan has ordered you to do. Now get on with it and then you can go home.'

Then she saw a mountain of books in front of her and the sunshine streaming in through the windows made the library look very alluring.

It was then she knew, if she was honest, that she had no wish to go home.

She wanted to stay in this enchanted castle.

However wrong it might be for her as a McKyle, she wanted to look at and go on talking to the Earl.

CHAPTER FIVE

Vanora heard the guests arriving the next afternoon.

They chatted as they walked from the hall up to the drawing room.

She wondered if amongst them there was anyone as beautiful as the lady whom Lady Sophie had mentioned as the Earl's last love in London.

She found herself thinking about it when she should have been sorting out the books.

Had the Earl missed her when he had returned to Scotland? Had he any intention of going back to London to be with her?

She wondered if the lady in question was clever as well as beautiful.

The more she had talked to the Earl, the more she realised how well read he was.

She was aware too that he had a 'third eye' which made him see deep inside the person he was speaking to.

Once or twice when they were having a discussion, she realised that he had read her thoughts before she had expressed them or he anticipated what she was going to say before she said it.

She tried not to think about him.

Yet her thoughts kept returning to the guests who were upstairs.

She found it hard to concentrate on the books.

There was one shelf right in the middle of the room that she had finished.

She had filled it with all the books she could find in Gaelic and those that referred to the history of Scotland and that at least would make it easy for any visitors to find what they required.

It was not, however, other readers she was thinking about but the Earl.

She knew that he, if no one else, would appreciate the library when it was finished and she wanted to ask him now what he thought of the shelf that she had already done.

Then she told herself firmly that she must behave in a more discreet manner.

Otherwise Lady Sophie might want her sent away before her task was finished.

Even as she thought that, she remembered that her real task was to find the Stone.

When she had found it, Ewen would expect her to take it to him and leave the library unfinished.

She worked until it was teatime and then one of the maids brought her some tea on a tray.

She thanked her and the girl said,

"They be a-talkin' their heads off in the drawin' room and it makes me think of how quiet it usually be here in The Castle."

Vanora wondered if that was what the Earl enjoyed.

She quickly ate what was brought her for tea and continued her work with the books.

She was just considering what the next shelf should contain when the door of the library opened.

The Earl came in.

And it seemed to Vanora as if her heart turned a somersault.

She told herself it was because he was smiling and looking pleased to see her.

"I am afraid I have neglected you, Miss Bruce," he said. "I know my aunt has told you that we have guests to stay and, as they have not been to The Castle for years, they are curious to see the improvements I intend to make."

He paused for a moment to look at the books.

Then he went on,

"They will wish to see the library and I am sure that they will be very impressed with what you have achieved already."

"As you see," Vanora replied, "I have finished one shelf, but there are a great many more to do."

The Earl walked to the shelf and looked at it.

"I see what you have done and that is splendid. It is exactly what I wanted and I will be able to find any book I require without having to climb from one end of the room to the other."

"Don't speak too soon, my Lord," Vanora replied. "There are, as you well know, thousands more waiting for my attention."

"I am aware of that and I am extremely grateful to you for what you are doing in such a sensible way. I know, of course, that it would be quite impossible for you to be anything else."

He was gazing at her as he spoke.

Despite herself, Vanora blushed and it made her look even lovelier than she was already.

The Earl now demanded impulsively,

"How is it possible that you can look like you do and at the same time know so much about history?"

Vanora was just about to answer him when the door opened and Donald announced,

"Major and Mrs. Morgan to see you, my Lord."

The Earl turned round in surprise.

Vanora saw two people come into the room. The man was middle-aged and the woman very much younger and quite pretty.

For a moment the Earl did not speak.

She knew that he was not sure who the newcomers were and then he exclaimed,

"It's Cyril! Surely it is Cyril!"

"You are quite right," the newcomer said advancing towards him. "I hoped you would not have forgotten the time we spent together in the Regiment before I was posted to India."

"Of course I have not forgotten you," the Earl said. "But I am surprised to see you and – "

He looked towards the woman who had come into the room with him.

"Let me introduce my wife, Alice," Major Morgan said.

The Earl shook her by the hand.

"We have arrived to impose on your hospitality," Major Morgan said, "since one of the wheels on our chaise has something wrong with it."

The Earl was listening and Major Morgan went on,

"I have shown it to one of the men in your stables and he said he could have it mended by tomorrow morning, but unfortunately not before."

The Earl smiled.

"Then of course, Cyril, you and your wife must stay here tonight and I am delighted to welcome you."

"That is very kind of you, Neil," the Major replied.

"So what are you doing in Scotland," he enquired, "and so far North?"

"We are on our way to visit some of my wife's relations," the Major replied. "We took a ship for some of the way and then decided to drive in the Highlands, which I have always wanted to visit."

"Well, I am delighted to have you. Now you must come upstairs to the drawing room where my aunt, Lady Sophie, is having tea with my other guests."

He did not introduce the newcomers to Vanora.

She had moved away while they were talking to the other end of the library.

She watched them go, the Earl towering above his friend and she thought that they were lucky to be joining the party and would doubtless have many reminiscences of the past to talk about.

When they had gone, the library seemed very quiet and Vanora felt lonely.

The sun was shining brightly outside and she had been working ever since luncheon.

She decided that she needed some fresh air.

She let herself out of a door that was not often used and found the garden looking even more enchanting than it had from the windows.

She wanted to walk towards the fountain.

Yet she knew, if she did so, anyone looking out of the drawing room windows would see her and that might be a mistake.

She turned away from the front of The Castle and moved through some trees down towards the sea.

Now she had a clear view of the bay where the Earl's yacht was anchored in a secluded spot.

As she looked at it, she wished that the Earl would take her on it, if only for a short distance.

She had been very impressed by the yacht that had brought her to Edinburgh, but she thought that the Earl's was infinitely superior.

She wondered if he would soon get bored with The Castle and want to travel to other parts of the world and it would be so tempting having a yacht ready to carry him anywhere he wished to go and she longed to be able to do the same.

She stayed by the sea and in the garden for what seemed a long time and then the shadows began to deepen and the sun was sinking lower in the sky.

She thought she should go back to her room and so let herself in through the same door.

As she then walked into the library, she saw to her surprise that the Earl was there and alone.

As he saw her, he exclaimed,

"I was wondering where you could possibly be and if perhaps you had suddenly decided to return to Mount Olympus and I should be unable to find you again."

Vanora smiled.

"I have been in the garden," she explained, "and down to the sea. It was all so beautiful that I am afraid I lost count of time."

She thought as she spoke it did not really matter when she came in.

Then the Earl said,

"I came to ask you if you would be very kind and dine with us tonight. We have just discovered when the newcomers arrived that we are thirteen."

"And that is not lucky!" Vanora exclaimed.

"My aunt and two other women in the party have said that nothing will make them challenge Fate by sitting at a table when there are thirteen present."

"And only one of them is supposed to die," Vanora ventured.

"I know that," the Earl replied, "but I have no great wish for it to be me at the moment."

"Of course not! You have too much to do in your life before you leave it," Vanora insisted.

The Earl raised his eyebrows.

"More than I am doing already?"

"But naturally," Vanora said without thinking, "as you have only just become Chieftain of your Clan. Every new Chieftain brings changes, fresh ideas and, of course, improvements."

"So that is what you are expecting me to do?" the Earl asked. "I had the idea that the Clan of the MacFiles was in perfect condition and it was quite unnecessary for me to interfere."

"If that is what you have been told, my Lord, it's untrue. I have never yet known a satisfied Elder or a Clansman who did not want something he had been unable to obtain from his last Chieftain."

The Earl chuckled.

"Now you are trying to frighten me and I have the uncomfortable feeling that you are right. So, Miss Bruce, it is essential that you should not make us thirteen at the table tonight."

"I am delighted to accept your invitation, my Lord, if only to save you and your guests from anything that might be accounted bad luck."

She glanced at the clock on the mantelpiece as she spoke and added,

"In which case I had better go and dress. I suppose that dinner is at eight o'clock, my Lord?"

"Eight o'clock precisely," the Earl replied. "And thank you for saying you will join us."

He walked towards the door as he spoke.

Vanora hastily closed the drawer of her desk and then she hurried upstairs.

The housekeeper had already been informed that she was dining in the dining room and a bath was ready for her in front of the fireplace.

She thought that the guests might realise that she had been invited as an afterthought, so she deliberately put on one of her more elegant gowns.

It had been very expensive and had been greatly admired at the ball when she had last worn it.

It was a ball given by one of her mother's friends and she had been invited not only to the ball itself but to the dinner that preceded it.

She remembered now that the gentlemen on either side of her had paid her endless compliments and her dance card was filled up even before the dinner party reached the ballroom.

A thought suddenly struck her as she was walking towards the drawing room.

There was just an off-chance that one of the people staying here tonight might have seen her in London and so would recognise her.

It was not likely, but she felt nervous and a little worried as a footman opened the drawing room door for her.

The room seemed full of people, but to her relief she quickly saw the Earl.

He looked magnificent in evening dress with lace at his throat and he was standing in front of the fireplace.

When she appeared, he walked forward and began,

"Now I must introduce you to my friends and it is very good of you, Miss Bruce, to join us."

When they moved into the dining room, the table looked spectacular. It was ornamented with silver goblets, which Vanora was certain had been in the family for many generations.

The food was really delicious and she thought no one could look more impressive or handsome than the Earl sitting at the head of the table.

She found that Major Morgan was on her right.

She had heard him say to the Earl that he had been in India and so she tactfully asked him about that country, saying that it was a place she had always wanted to visit.

He was, she thought, somewhat reluctant to talk about India.

She did not know why, but she thought that there was something about the Major that was unpleasant and she could not explain it even to herself.

But she was using her 'third eye' which was what the Earl used.

Her instinct told her at once that Major Morgan was not only an unpleasant man but an untruthful one.

It was with a sense of relief that she talked to the gentleman on her other side and found that he had come to Scotland because he wanted to catch his first salmon and shoot his first stag.

"I have fished quite a lot in the South," he said, "but I am told that our host's river is filled with salmon and I want to be able to boast that I have caught a large number of them."

Vanora smiled.

"That is what everyone hopes. The rivers are doing well at the moment and I am sure you will be successful."

"If I shoot my first stag," he said proudly, "and it has a fine head, I will have it mounted."

"And your children, when you have them, will look at it enviously," Vanora said, "and try to shoot an even bigger one!"

"I know that is true," he replied. "It is what I felt about my father's first stag's head when I first saw it. I think I was three or four at the time."

"And you waited all this while before coming to Scotland?" Vanora asked.

"I was with the Army of Occupation in France and then, when my Regiment returned, I did not have the time to come to Scotland. But now, thanks to an invitation from our host, I am delighted to be here."

"And I can only wish you every success," Vanora replied. "I am sure that you will find Scotland as exciting as most sportsmen do."

The young gentleman raised his glass.

"Thank you for that and may I say that you are far too lovely to be a Scot and, if you are, it is London's loss!"

Vanora laughed.

As she did so, she realised from the top of the table that the Earl was looking at her.

She wished that she was sitting next to him and she had the absurd idea that he was thinking the same.

Then she told herself firmly that she was just being imaginative.

The two women on either side of him were well-dressed and, although not especially beautiful, they were attractive and obviously amusing to talk to.

She had been aware that the Earl was laughing and they were laughing too, but she was too far down the table to hear what was being said.

As was usual in Scotland, and had always happened when Vanora was at her home, the Chieftain's piper played round the table as dinner ended.

He had started to fill his bag down the passage and they heard the first notes very faintly in the distance.

And then the sound of the pipes grew louder and louder until he entered the room and he was a tall good-looking man and, of course, he was wearing the MacFile tartan.

First he played one of the special tunes of the Clan.

Then, as he started *Over the Sea to Skye*, Vanora felt tears come into her eyes as it was a tune that always moved her.

It always upset her and made her unhappy to think how nearly successful Bonnie Prince Charlie had been and how many people had subsequently suffered because they believed in him and had gladly followed him.

As the notes rang out, she looked up the table and could see that the Earl was watching her.

She had a strong feeling that he understood what she was thinking and again she was almost certain that he felt the same.

Then the piper played a more cheerful tune until finally he stopped beside the Earl's chair.

As was traditional, the Earl took a small silver cup from the table. It was filled with whisky and so the piper accepted it.

He raised the glass to the Earl and called out,

"*Slainte Var!*"

Then he drank.

The Earl thanked him and all the guests applauded before the piper left the room.

After that Lady Sophie rose and took the ladies into the drawing room.

Vanora found that they not only admired her gown but were very curious as to who she was.

She was nervous that they might ask her questions that it would be difficult for her to answer, so she went to the window to look out at the moon and the stars shining over the sea.

She was still standing a little way away from the other women in the party when the gentlemen joined them.

Card tables had been arranged at one end of the drawing room and it was obvious that bridge was what the gentlemen wanted to play.

The women gathered round the fire which had just been lit as, although it was summer, there was generally a chill wind from the sea after dark.

It was then that Vanora felt it would be easy for her to slip away from the party.

The Earl had by now seated himself at one of the card tables with three other men who were staying in the house.

Several women moved in to watch the game.

One woman in particular, who Vanora had heard called Lady Ruth, was leaning over the Earl's shoulder. She was quite the most attractive of the guests.

She was also whispering in his ear and it occurred to Vanora that perhaps Lady Sophie had asked her because she wanted her nephew to be married.

The Earl seemed to be listening to what she said and the two of them with their heads close together made, Vanora thought, a pretty picture.

'There is no reason for me to stay,' she told herself.

She managed to move slowly towards the door.

Then, when everyone was talking to someone else, she slipped out without saying goodnight.

She told herself it would be a mistake to outstay her welcome and she had done what they wanted of her.

And anyway she was not really one of the party but merely someone useful.

When she reached her bedroom, she undressed and then she stood for a long time at the window.

It was not so much that she was thinking. She was just seeing the beauty that lay before her and letting it seep into her soul.

'This is my Scotland and where I belong,' she told herself.

Yet, although she could not put it into words, she wanted more, so much more that she felt that she would never attain it however hard she tried.

It was quite late when she finally climbed into bed.

Even so she found it hard to sleep and lay awake thinking of the books downstairs and how much more there was to do.

She had found one book today that she was longing to discuss with the Earl, but she was not certain whether he would have the time.

It was 'The Essays of Francis Bacon,' a first edition published in 1597, which contained ten essays.

She was sure that it was extremely valuable and she also wanted to ask the Earl if there was any chance of the second and third editions being in the library.

It was then when she was thinking about the books that she remembered something.

She had left the catalogue she was making of them on her desk and it was not locked away.

She appreciated better than the Earl how valuable the books were and it would be wrong to let anyone see her catalogue and steal the books before she had time to finish identifying them.

On other nights she had locked her catalogue away and she also locked the door of the library before she went upstairs.

Tonight, because she was thinking about the dinner party, she had omitted both precautions.

Getting out of bed she pulled on her dressing gown, which was a very pretty satin one trimmed with an ancient lace she had bought at a bazaar.

She picked up the candle by her bed that was small and not too heavy.

Letting herself out of her room, she went down the long passage. Then to the staircase that led to the far end of The Castle where the library was situated.

Everything was very quiet.

Venora thought that by now the house party must have gone to their rooms and in any case they were some way away from where she slept.

She went into the library and found as she expected that she had left her catalogue on the desk.

It was obvious that no one had touched it, but she told herself that it was something she should not do again.

She started to tidy up her pens and pieces of paper she had used to make notes.

Suddenly she could hear the sound of someone approaching.

She had no wish to be found in the library in only her dressing gown by a servant or by anyone else.

Quickly and instinctively she blew out the candle she had placed on the writing desk and then she slipped behind the curtains of one of the long windows.

In the window there was a window seat upholstered in the same damask as the curtains.

Vanora climbed up onto the seat and stood holding together the curtains in front of her and she was scared that they might fall open to reveal her presence.

She heard someone come into the library and then she realised that it was not one person but two.

She heard them shut the door behind them and then, as she held her breath, they seemed to walk towards her.

They came near and a man's voice said,

"Now you start here looking where Harry told you and I will cope with the picture."

Even as the man spoke she recognised his voice.

It was Major Morgan.

There was a pause before his wife Alice replied,

"Harry told us that 'the Folio' was on the top shelf. I shall have to go up onto the balcony."

There was silence for a moment and then Major Morgan said,

"I think the steps are on the other side. You should have no difficulty."

Vanora heard them walk across the room.

Then, when she was certain that they were some distance from her, she gently opened the two curtains she was holding and peeped through the gap.

She saw that the Morgans had brought two candles with them and one was on the floor near the mantelpiece.

To her horror she could see Major Morgan lifting down the portrait painted by Holbein.

Vanora had already ascertained when in the library that the picture was a portrait of the fourth Earl of Glenfile and there had been no need for anyone to tell her how valuable it was.

Even as she peeped at Major Morgan, she saw his wife coming round the balcony and going to the far end where the shelves were full of books that Vanora had not yet had time to investigate.

Now she saw that Mrs. Morgan was pulling out the books from the top shelf and putting them down carelessly on the floor of the balcony.

Vanora knew without even questioning what they had meant when they said 'the Folio'.

They were undoubtedly referring to the *First Folio* of Shakespeare which she had been hoping to find.

Her eyes were once again on Major Morgan.

He now had the frame containing the Holbein down on the floor and was taking the picture out of the frame.

The frame itself was clearly old and valuable and she wondered why he did not take it at the same time as the picture.

Then, as he freed it comparatively easily from the frame, she saw him reach towards a black bag he had put down on the floor beside the candle.

Only as he drew something from it did she realise what he intended to do.

He had a replica of Holbein's portrait, which he intended to substitute in the frame.

No one, unless they were very observant and very knowledgeable, would realise what had happened and in the meantime he would then be in possession of the real Holbein.

Vanora drew in her breath at the idea of it being stolen and doubtless lost for ever.

She peeped again at what Alice Morgan was doing.

She had moved all the volumes at the end of the top shelf onto the floor of the balcony and now she reached out her hand and gave a little cry of excitement.

"I have found it! I have found it, Cyril!"

She spoke in a whisper but it carried to her husband in the empty room.

"Good," he replied. "Harry will be delighted. Of course we shall have to give him a share of the spoils."

"But not too big a share," Alice said sharply. "And I have also found the Chaucer he told us about."

"Splendid!" Major Morgan exclaimed. "Is it the edition we wanted?"

Alice had to bend down towards her candle which was on the floor of the balcony.

"It is entitled *The Workes of Geoffrey Chaucer*," she said, "published by W. Thynne."

"That's it," Major Morgan crowed, "and, when I have put this picture back, the sooner we get out of here the better."

"Does it really look like the original?" Alice asked.

"It's the spitting image of it," her husband replied. "You can always trust those Indians to do a good job when it comes to painting or carving."

"Then if you have finished," Alice said, "come and help me put back these books because they are heavy and I am tired."

"I will," Major Morgan replied.

As he spoke, he lifted up the frame with the false picture in it over the mantelpiece.

It was difficult to see at a distance and Vanora was almost certain that the average person would not notice any difference when they came into the library.

'People see just what they expect to see,' she told herself.

She knew it was very clever of the Major to have brought a substitute for the Holbein he was stealing.

If she had not been here by accident, no one coming in or out of the library would have looked twice at the Holbein picture to see if it was real.

It was a different story where the Shakespeare *First Folio* and the *Workes of Chaucer* were concerned.

It might have been weeks or even months before she would have reached the books on the top shelf.

Now Major Morgan was climbing onto the balcony by the steps that were out of sight.

But a few moments later he came round to where Vanora could see him and helped his wife.

He put all the books back into the shelves.

Then they both stood for a moment looking at the picture over the mantelpiece.

"It might be years," Alice Morgan said, "before anyone realises that is not the real McCoy."

"The longer the better where we are concerned," Major Morgan murmured.

He picked up the black bag in which he had put the stolen Holbein.

"Now come along," he said. "We have earned our sleep and we will leave as soon as possible after breakfast."

"Make sure of that," Alice urged. "The sooner we get away from here the better."

They walked towards the door, opened it and going out, closed it quietly behind them.

For a moment Vanora did not move as there was always a chance that the two thieves might turn back.

If they saw her, she had the feeling that she would not live long to talk about it.

At the same time every nerve in her body was crying out at what she had just witnessed.

She knew that there was only one thing she could do about it.

Slowly, because she was still frightened, she pulled open the curtains and stepped onto the floor.

The candle she had brought was still on the writing table and the moonlight showed her where it was and how she could light it.

Then silently she moved across the floor towards the door and, because she was still afraid, she listened for a moment before she opened it.

Again, after she had turned the handle, she listened.

Everything was quiet and the passage outside was in complete darkness.

It did not take her long to reach the staircase that led up to the first floor.

Here there was no longer any need for her candle as the corridor was dimly lit and she blew it out.

She reached her own room and then hesitated.

There was only one person who could cope with the situation and she had to tell him.

She put down her candle and started to run along the passage.

It led to the State room where the Earl slept.

She knew where it was.

She had had a quick peep in the rooms when she had been looking for the housekeeper and had found her in the Chieftain's bedroom with two of the housemaids.

When she spoke to her, the housekeeper had come at once to the door and over her shoulder Vanora had seen the magnificent canopied Chieftain's bed.

It was carved and painted in gold and other colours and the curtains were dark crimson. Behind the bedhead was a Coat of Arms exquisitely embroidered on velvet.

That was where the Earl would be sleeping now.

If she was to save his possessions, Vanora knew that she must tell him immediately what she had seen.

Only as she reached the door did she hesitate before she opened it.

Then resolutely, because nothing mattered but the theft of three irreplaceable treasures, she went in.

She expected the room to be in darkness, but the Earl had pulled back the curtains before he went to sleep and the moon was now pouring a silver light in through the windows.

It was easy to make out the outline of the bedposts and the bed itself.

Vanora reached it.

Then, silent though she had been, her very presence stirred the Earl.

He moved, opened his eyes and stared at her.

"Who is it?" he asked. "What do you want?"

Now the Earl could see the moon turning Vanora's hair to silver and its light glowing behind her as if it was an aura.

For a moment it was impossible to speak.

Then he exclaimed incredulously,

"Miss Bruce! What is the matter? Why are you here?"

Vanora was sure that they were a long way away from where anyone could hear them and yet she did not want to take a chance.

So she went down on her knees beside the bed.

"A terrible thing has happened," she began. "Your friends who arrived tonight – Major Morgan and his wife – have stolen the portrait by Holbein – from the library and also the Shakespeare *First Folio* – and a book by Chaucer."

For a moment the Earl was speechless and then he demanded,

"However do you know this?"

Vanora drew in her breath.

"I went to the library because I forgot – when you asked me to dinner, to put away the catalogue I have been compiling of the books. I thought it would be a mistake for anyone to see it and – what I have already discovered."

She stopped for a moment as she was breathless.

Then the Earl said quietly,

"Go on."

"I had just reached the library," Vanora continued, "when I heard someone coming. I blew out my candle and hid – behind the curtains in one of the windows."

The Earl moved himself up a little higher on his pillows as if he was afraid of missing anything.

"Then I heard someone come into the library," she went on, "and when I peeped through the curtains I saw – Major Morgan and his wife."

"They were fully dressed?" the Earl enquired.

"Yes, but not in the same clothes they were wearing at dinner – just easy things to slip on."

Vanora had not thought of this at the time, but now she continued,

"He was carrying a black bag with him and he took down the portrait by Holbein – from over the mantelpiece."

"I cannot believe it," the Earl murmured.

"Mrs. Morgan," Vanora went on, "said that Harry had told her where – 'the Folio' was hidden."

"Harry?" the Earl questioned.

"Yes – that was who she said."

"Then I know who you mean. Harry Henderson. He was a friend of my father and took, I believe, quite a lot of money off him. But do go on."

"Harry had apparently told them that he had hidden 'the Folio' at the far end of the highest shelf – above the balcony."

"I am sure it's the last place that you would have looked," the Earl remarked.

"I was doing the lower shelves first."

"And she found the *First Folio* there?"

"That and the Chaucer were there hidden behind the other books on the shelf."

The Earl gave a sudden exclamation.

"I remember now," he said, "I was here when Harry last came to stay with my father not very long before his death. In fact I was home from school."

"Did you know he was a crook?" Vanora asked.

"No, but my father did. I do remember him saying when Harry left, 'I hurried him off because I was quite certain that, if I left him alone for a minute, he would put something in his pocket and we would never see it again'."

Vanora gave a little sigh.

"What he had intended to take with him was the Shakespeare *First Folio* and the Chaucer."

"I know that now," the Earl replied. "But Harry was never asked again to The Castle, so he had to employ the Morgans to steal the treasures he had left behind."

"And now you must stop them taking them."

"Of course," the Earl agreed. "At the same time I do *not* want a scandal. If the house party talks, we shall have a whole spate of burglars breaking in here one way or another."

Vanora was silent for a moment and then she said,

"I have an idea which I think will help if you would agree to it."

CHAPTER SIX

"I am listening," the Earl said, "but I think that you would be more comfortable if you sat on the bed."

Vanora did as she was told and sat down a little way from him.

This meant that he could see her silhouetted against the moonlight and she looked even more ethereal than she usually did.

The Earl was now sitting up almost straight against his pillows.

Vanora began slowly,

"I was thinking that the Morgans said they were going to leave soon after breakfast. If it was possible for you to delay them by offering to take them somewhere for the morning, I could put the real Holbein back in its frame and the fake in their bag."

The Earl made an exclamation, but did not interrupt her and Vanora went on,

"Also, if the books are wrapped up, I could change the two precious ones for something – you do not want."

She spoke a little hesitatingly.

The Earl listened to the end and then cried,

"That is such a brilliant idea and only *you* could have thought of it!"

"I am sure, because they are so certain that no one would notice that the portrait has been changed," Vanora said, "the real Holbein will still be in the black bag where Major Morgan put it, in his bedroom."

"And the books will doubtless be in her luggage," the Earl suggested.

There was silence and then he went on,

"You may have to take the housekeeper into your confidence, but it is essential that the young maidservants should not be told. They would undoubtedly gossip in the village."

"If you take the Morgans away immediately after breakfast," Vanora said, "it is most unlikely, since they are leaving for good that their rooms will be done very early. I know that housemaids in most houses attend to the more important guests first."

"Then let's hope they do so on this occasion," the Earl said.

As he sat looking at Vanora, he thought again how exquisite she was and it was hard to realise how intelligent.

Then, as if she was still thinking it all out, Vanora said,

"There is another point. As I am not as strong as the Major, I may have difficulty in lifting the portrait down from the wall."

"I had not thought of that," the Earl said, "but, of course, you are right. What we had better do is to go to the library now and I will take the Holbein down. There will be no one about at this time of night."

"Everything was quiet when I left the library."

"Then I suggest," the Earl said, "that to spare your blushes you go and look out of the window while I get out of bed."

Without saying anything Vanora slipped off the bed and walked to the window.

She thought as she gazed out how peaceful it all seemed. It was hard to believe that human beings planned to commit horrible crimes when nature itself was just so glorious.

She heard the Earl moving about the room behind her and then he said,

"I am ready now."

She turned round and saw that he had put on a long dark robe rather like the one her uncle had always worn. It was frogged with braid and gave the wearer a somewhat military appearance.

The Earl was lighting the candle beside his bed and then, as he walked towards the door, Vanora followed him.

Without speaking they went down the long passage.

As they neared the library, Vanora was suddenly afraid that the Morgans might have come back to find other spoils and perhaps when they reached their bedroom they had thought that they had been too hasty in not searching for more treasures.

But there was no sound as they neared the door and, when the Earl opened it, the great room was in darkness.

He walked to the fireplace and held up his candle.

He could now see the portrait of his ancestor quite clearly.

Vanora had not spent time looking at the original and yet she knew that the copy that Major Morgan had inserted into the frame would have deceived her.

As if the Earl knew what she was thinking, he said,

"I have to admit it is cleverly done."

"That is what I was thinking," Vanora said. "You might not have noticed the difference for a very long time."

"And that is what they were hoping would happen," the Earl said grimly.

He handed Vanora the candle.

Then he reached forward to lift down the portrait from over the mantelpiece.

It was, he realised, far too heavy for a woman, as he lowered it gently against one of the armchairs.

"I will undo the back for you," he said, "if you can give me something to do it with."

Vanora put the candle down and ran to her desk.

She knew that she did not have any special tool, but there was a pair of scissors and a silver letter opener.

She carried them to the Earl, who had turned the picture round and was examining the back.

"It is really quite simple," he said. "I suppose to save himself trouble he has fastened it in only two places."

"That will make it easier for me to do the same," Vanora said and the Earl smiled.

"I cannot imagine you being defeated by anything, least of all a thief."

She gave a little cry.

"Touch wood! They may cheat you in some other way and we must be very much on our guard."

"I am going to risk," the Earl said, "anyone coming into the library before you do in the morning."

For a moment Vanora did not know what he meant and then she saw him take the fake out of its frame. He placed it on the seat of the chair propping it against the back.

"All you have to do," the Earl said, "is to put the real Holbein back into the frame and then, if it's possible, attend to the books."

"Everything depends on your keeping them away from The Castle while I do it," Vanora answered. "If I must not fail, neither must you."

"I think Fate and the angels who look after you," he said, "are working overtime. It was just by chance that you should have been in the library when those devils came in to despoil me."

He paused before he went on,

"Do you realise that if they had not been so greedy as to take the Holbein as well as the books, I should never have been aware of what I had lost."

"I had not thought of that, my Lord, but then it does seem rather stupid of them."

"What I would like to see," the Earl said, "is the expression on their faces when they reach their destination and become aware of what has happened."

"They deserve everything that happens to them and in fact they will have been let off very lightly."

"That is true," the Earl answered. "But it would be a great mistake for anyone to learn of what has occurred."

Vanora agreed with him and then the Earl picked up the candle.

He took a last look at the fake Holbein and walked to the door.

As she followed him, Vanora was wondering if she should tell him of the book by John Dryden she had found.

Then she thought it would be a mistake when his mind was on the two volumes that had been stolen.

When they were outside the library, the Earl locked the door and handed her the key.

She did not say anything, but she knew that it was the sensible thing to do, as no one could enter now until she had opened the door in the morning.

They walked up the stairs in silence and only when they reached Vanora's bedroom did the Earl speak.

"I don't know how to thank you," he said in a low voice, "for being brave enough to come and tell me what has happened and to help me, as you are doing, to get back my treasures."

"I am praying that everything will go smoothly," Vanora whispered. "Please try to keep them away as long as you can, in case I have any difficulties in getting into their rooms."

"I will carry out your orders to the letter," the Earl said with a faint smile. "In fact what I intend to do is to take them out in my yacht, telling them it is important they should see The Castle from the sea or something like that."

"Supposing they refuse," Vanora murmured.

"If they do so, I will make it almost impossible for them without being exceedingly rude," the Earl replied.

He thought for a moment and then went on,

"I will also, now I think of it, send for one of the men who are mending the wheel of their chaise and tell him to try it out first to make sure that it will not collapse again on the journey."

Vanora clapped her hands together.

"That is brilliant of you, my Lord, and now I don't feel so afraid."

"That is something I have no wish for you to feel and thank you again for being so wonderful."

He bent forward and to her astonishment kissed her cheek.

It was only a light kiss, but, as his lips touched her skin, she felt a little quiver go through her.

The Earl walked away without looking back and she stood watching him until he was out of sight.

Only as she went into her bedroom did she put her hand to her cheek.

How amazing it was.

He had kissed her!

She had come to The Castle to carry out Ewen's orders and never had she dreamt for a single moment that she would be in any way intimate with the Earl.

Or that he would treat her as he would treat a woman in the same Social world as himself.

She was just an employee.

Now incredibly she was saving the Earl's treasures!

But she still had no idea at all where the Stone was hidden or even perhaps that it still existed.

That thought had not occurred to her before.

Now she was wondering to herself if perhaps the Earl's father, disliking the McKyle Clan as much as they disliked him, had thrown it into the sea or maybe he had buried it in the garden.

Whatever the answer might be, it was the Stone that had brought her here, the Stone that had made it possible for her not only to handle the books that were a thrill in themselves but to meet their owner.

'He has kissed my cheek,' she told herself as she stood in the moonlight.

It was the way that he would have expressed his gratitude to any woman who had helped him.

Yet it was something she would always remember.

She climbed into bed by the light from the window, knowing it was vital that she should wake early.

She must know immediately when the Earl took the Morgans away from the Castle.

She had closed her eyes and said a prayer when she had first got into bed.

Now she found it impossible to sleep.

In another part of The Castle, the Earl was awake as well.

He had gone into his room thinking it extraordinary for any man to be involved in such a drama.

How could he have ever imagined when he came back to Scotland that one of the most valuable pictures in The Castle would have been replaced.

And by a copy made in India, presumably from an illustration of it in some book.

It was only, as he thought, by a miracle that he was made aware of it.

What was more the Shakespeare *First Folio* which he had begun to doubt really existed and a precious edition of Chaucer were actually in The Castle, but not now in his hands.

He could imagine the satisfaction what the Morgans were now feeling. They had pulled off most skilfully a well thought-out plan.

Of course the broken wheel was a fake and Major Morgan had relied on his acquaintance with the Earl when they were in the Regiment together to gain his hospitality.

Now he thought about it, the Earl remembered that Morgan had done something wrong. He could not recall what it was, but it had brought the wrath of the Colonel down on his head and Morgan had been transferred.

The Earl reflected now that it must have been the real reason for him being transferred to another Regiment in India.

'I should have been suspicious of him at the time,' he told himself, 'but it all happened such a long time ago.'

He had entirely forgotten Morgan until he appeared and asked for his hospitality.

'It was all a wicked trick,' the Earl thought angrily, 'and if it had not been for Miss Bruce they would have left tomorrow and I would never have seen them again.'

He began to ponder on how clever Miss Bruce had been.

It was impossible to think of anything, except how lovely she looked with the moonlight touching her hair.

She had looked, he thought, perhaps even lovelier in the light of the candle that he was carrying when they reached her bedroom.

He had looked down at her and she was very small beside him and he thought there was something irresistible about her.

Once again he hardly believed that she was real.

He had kissed her in sincere gratitude, just as he would have kissed any other woman who had helped him.

Yet when his lips touched her skin he had known, although he could not put it into words, that what he felt was very different from anything he had ever felt before.

'I am just imagining it,' he now told himself in the darkness.

But he could see her clearly in a hundred different aspects, particularly sitting at her desk in the library and walking into the drawing room with a grace that no other woman could boast.

He had thought at dinner that she eclipsed everyone else at the table and he was well aware that it was difficult for the other men to take their eyes away from her.

Yet curiously and to him quite incomprehensively, she appeared completely unconscious of her beauty.

Again he was thinking that she could not be real.

How could she have lived in London with anyone as influential as Lord Blairmond and not had dozens of men at her feet?

'If she is really unspoilt,' he told himself, 'then it is a miracle.'

But whatever way he twisted it, she still remained, he decided, unaware of him as a man. She was interested only in The Castle and its possessions.

The Earl thought of Vanora and went on thinking about her.

Then it flashed through his mind that it would be a disaster if he fell in love with her.

How could he possibly, in his position, offer her marriage? Yet he was convinced that she would be shocked and horrified at the suggestion of anything else.

In London, as he knew only too well, love was a word that covered a multitude, if not of sins, then of those situations that were secret and covered up.

It was rather strange, but he was utterly convinced of something in his very astute mind.

It was what Miss Bruce was looking for in life, the love that had always evaded him.

Which in fact he had begun to think did not really exist except in Fairytales.

Practically every book, he thought cynically, in the library would have been written about the real love that he could not find.

Yet despite himself he was idealistic and deep in his heart he believed that one day he would find love.

The love men had fought for, suffered and died for all through history. The majority had been disappointed and yet led by the Bethlehem Star they had never ceased to seek it.

If he was truthful with himself, that was what he wanted, the real love of a man for a woman and a woman for a man.

It was sacred and was as near as a human could get to the love of God.

He supposed, now he thought of it, that this was what his dear mother must have planted in his mind when he was very young.

It had been there ever since, although it was only now that he was actually aware of it.

It was all because he had met this girl and he was convinced that she was completely different from any other woman who had come into his life.

He was still thinking of Vanora when he fell asleep.

*

He felt that he had not been asleep for long when his valet was pulling back the curtains.

The sun instead of the full moon was streaming in through the windows.

The Earl jumped out of bed and, as soon as he was dressed, went into the breakfast room and because he was early there was no one else present.

He then sat down at the top of the table where a newspaper was propped up on a silver stand for him.

Major Morgan and his wife then came hurrying into the room.

"Good morning, Cyril," the Earl said in a hearty voice. "You are early."

"We want to be on our way as soon as possible," Major Morgan said, "although it is sad to leave you, Neil, and we have enjoyed every moment of our visit here."

"I am pleased to hear it, Cyril, and you must come again and stay much longer. Perhaps it would be possible on your way South."

"We will certainly think about it," he replied.

He went to the sideboard and his wife followed him. There were a number of dishes including, of course, porridge.

The Earl had already eaten some from the wooden bowl bearing his initials that he had used since a child and the Morgans now helped themselves to bacon and eggs and sat down at the table.

"I think your carriage will be ready in an hour or so," the Earl said. "But I have given orders that it should be tried out by one of my grooms to make sure that it does not break down again when you are on the road."

"I certainly hope it will not do that," Alice Morgan said. "And we are so lucky that when it broke yesterday we were so close to your lovely castle."

"And I was lucky in being able to catch up with an old friend again," the Earl said. "And that reminds me. I remember, Cyril, how interested you were in all different kinds of mechanisms and so I want you to see, before you leave, the new improvements I have made to my yacht."

"I saw your yacht in the bay," he remarked.

"What I suggest," the Earl went on, "is that you and your wife come aboard when you have finished breakfast. I will ask the Captain to move us a little way out to sea so that you can see how my new engines work."

"That would be very interesting," Major Morgan said, "but unfortunately – "

The Earl held up his hands.

"I will not take 'no' for an answer. The groom has only just left to carry out the trial I insisted upon for your chaise. It will be ready when I bring you back from our little sea voyage."

It was obvious that Major Morgan was reluctant to do what the Earl had suggested.

He stole a quick glance at his wife.

"Of course we will come and see your yacht," she said," but you must promise that you will not make us late because we have a long way to go."

"I promise," the Earl replied, "and, although I don't want to hurry you over your breakfast, the sooner we are started the quicker we will be back."

Alice Morgan laughed.

Then the Earl said,

"I have already told the Captain that we shall be coming aboard. We only have to walk down the garden to do so."

The Morgans finished their breakfast and, as soon as they had done so, the Earl rose to his feet.

"Come along," he urged, "and, Cyril, I particularly want your opinion on my new gadgets. I am sure that you will have plenty of ideas for further improvements."

"I cannot be sure of that," Major Morgan replied. "But I think you are extremely lucky to have such a fine yacht."

"Then you must promise to come for a trip with me, perhaps to the Orkneys, on your next visit," the Earl said cheerily. "Although I daresay that your wife would find Denmark more amusing."

"You make it sound so fascinating," Alice Morgan added, "and we will not forget your invitation."

She looked at her husband as she spoke.

The Earl was then aware that Major Morgan looked surreptitiously at his watch before they followed him.

He led the way down the stairs and into the garden.

There were steps leading down to the fountain and they walked quite a little way further to where there was a long wooden pier jutting out into the bay.

At the end of it the Earl's yacht was waiting with a gangway laid down on the pier.

The Captain welcomed them aboard.

As they started to move away out towards the sea, the Earl looked back at The Castle.

Some of his other guests who were late coming down to breakfast were waving to him from one of the windows.

He knew that Donald would have told them where he had gone.

He waved back and Alice Morgan said,

"I expect they would have liked to come with us."

"I remembered you were anxious to leave early," the Earl replied, "and I can easily take them another day."

He thought that the Morgans seemed satisfied with his explanation.

They were now moving out of the bay into the open sea and the Earl saw the Major looking once again at his watch.

*

From her bedroom window Vanora saw the Earl and the Morgans walking down the garden.

She was, however, going to take no chances of their coming back at the last moment.

She waited until she saw the yacht begin to move.

Then she had hurried first to the Morgans' bedroom which was not too far from her own.

As she had hoped and prayed, there was no sign of a housemaid.

A trunk was in the bedroom and Alice Morgan's nightgown was lying on the bed and her hairbrushes and combs were still on the dressing table.

Vanora had been afraid that she might have packed all her belongings and locked the trunk and she would then have had to force the lock to open it.

She looked around and saw that Alice's dressing gown was lying on a chair and Vanora realised that they were too clever to make even the housemaids suspicious that they had anything to hide.

It would be quite unthinkable for any guest at The Castle to pack for themselves and the Morgans were aware of this.

The dressing room that opened out of the bedroom was where Major Morgan's trunk would be and that too, Vanora hoped, would not be fastened.

She locked the door and then going quickly to Mrs. Morgan's trunk she knelt down beside it.

It was filled with clothes and toiletries that had not been unpacked.

She soon found a hard lump at the very bottom of the trunk that was in the shape of a book.

She pulled it out to find that it had been wrapped in tissue paper and tied with a bow of blue ribbon.

It gave the impression that it might be a present, perhaps for her hostess at the next house they would stay in.

It took Vanora only a second or so to open it.

She saw as she expected that it was *The Workes of Geoffrey Chaucer* published in 1532.

She felt a throb of relief when she saw the title and quickly she took up two of the books she had brought with her.

She covered them with the tissue paper and tied them, as the Chaucer book had been, with the blue ribbon.

When she put it back into the trunk, she found that Shakespeare's *First Folio* was lying beside it.

121

She thought when she saw it that it was larger than she had expected and, although she put two books in its place, it did not take up as much room as the *First Folio*.

She only hoped that Mrs. Morgan would not look before they left The Castle to see if what she had stolen was safe.

It was rather unlikely and anyway by the time they had returned from the yacht their luggage would have been picked up and taken downstairs by the footmen.

Holding the precious *First Folio* and the Chaucer in her hands, Vanora went to the dressing room that the Major had used.

His trunk was open on the floor.

Even as she looked at it her heart gave a leap.

Propped up against the wall beside it there was the black bag that he had been carrying last night.

There was no need to look to see what it contained.

She then picked the black bag up and, going back into Mrs. Morgan's room, she opened the door that she had locked.

There was no one in sight and yet she could hear some servants or it might be guests talking in a room two or three doors away.

Quietly she closed the door and then she ran down the passage and down the staircase and on to the library.

She had the key in her pocket and pulled it out.

When she entered, the curtains were drawn and it would have been impossible to get in even if the servants had tried to open up the room.

The copy of Holbein's portrait lay just as the Earl had left it.

It took her only a few seconds to take out the real picture from the black bag and she slipped the copy into it.

Vanora was still worried that the Morgans might somehow get hold of the books she had taken from Alice's bedroom.

She therefore pulled several volumes out of the nearest shelf and pushed the *First Folio* and the Chaucer behind them, just as Harry had done years ago.

Now she had only to take the bag back into Major Morgan's room.

She had worked quickly and yet she was terrified that the Morgans would persuade the Earl to return quicker than he intended.

She ran up the staircase and along the passage.

She entered Alice Morgan's bedroom.

Then she was aware that the door of the dressing room was open and there was a footman inside it.

He was obviously packing the Major's clothes.

For a moment Vanora stood still trying frantically to think what she should do.

Then she did the only sensible thing that would not cause any commotion.

She pulled open the door.

As she expected, the footman was kneeling on the floor by Major Morgan's trunk, packing his evening suit.

"Good morning, Gordon," Vanora said.

"Good morning, miss," Gordon replied.

"His Lordship asked me to bring this bag back to Major Morgan," Vanora said. "It belongs to him, but he was showing his Lordship something that was in it. Do be careful not to leave it behind when you take the luggage downstairs."

"I'll not forget, miss," Gordon smiled. "And how be you getting' on with them books?"

Vanora smiled at him.

"Very well," she replied. "But, as you know, there are a great number of them and to make things perfect it is going to be a very long job."

"I'll bet it be," Gordon said.

Vanora laughed and left him.

As she walked to her own room, she felt suddenly limp. The effort of doing everything so quickly had almost sapped her strength.

She went to the window and now she could see that the yacht was still some way out to sea and it looked quite small against the horizon.

'I need not have been frightened,' she told herself.

The Earl had been clever in making sure that there was no chance of them returning too soon.

She went down again to the library.

She looked at the portrait by Holbein, which was lying on the chair in front of the empty frame where the Earl had placed it.

Deftly she put the canvas back into it and she fixed it in almost the same way as it had been before.

Then she turned it round and could see that it was so finely painted and knew at once that it would have been a tragedy if it had fallen into the Morgans' hands.

It would doubtless have been sold later to some museum for a very large sum of money.

She knew that it was too heavy for her to lift back into place and she hoped that the Earl would remember and put it back for her.

At the same time, if any of the servants came in, she was ready with an explanation – the Earl had taken it down because he thought it was not as securely fastened as it should have been.

'I have thought of everything,' she told herself with a little sigh.

She did not take the *First Folio* or the Chaucer from the hiding place where she had put them. That could wait until the Morgans had left and she had the Earl alone.

She wanted to see his delight when he saw the *First Folio* for the very first time. He would then know that it really existed and was not just a legend handed down the centuries.

'He is very very lucky,' she told herself.

She went to the writing desk and then remembered once again the reason why she was at The Castle.

She had been so intent on working on the books for the last few days that she had made no effort to find the Stone.

She had also completely forgotten that Ewen was sending a man to wait at the end of the wood every night in case she had a message for him.

'He will have to wait,' she told herself. 'As I have no news, there is no point in talking to him and having to walk through the wood in the dark.'

She did, however, think that she should now make an effort to find the Stone.

She left the library and went into one or two rooms that she had not yet seen and she had learned from Lady Sophie and the housekeeper that they were not often in use.

There were plenty of stags' heads, a great number of valuable pictures, but no sign of a Stone.

In one room there were the Peers' robes that the Earl's grandparents had worn at the Opening of Parliament.

In another there were a number of old fish hooks and Vanora was to learn later that making them had been a hobby of one of the Earl's relatives.

In addition there were many small objects that she found fascinating, like antique snuffboxes, a collection of pewter mugs and some very lovely pieces of porcelain.

Still there was no sign of the Stone.

She thought by this time that the Morgans must be on their way back to The Castle.

When she looked out of a window again, she saw them disembarking from the yacht onto the pier.

She thought that it would be a mistake for them to see her or for her to be anywhere but in the library where she belonged.

She hurried back there.

If it was not for the Holbein portrait propped up on the armchair, she would have thought that what happened last night had been just a dream.

*

The Earl had managed to keep his guests well away from The Castle for over an hour and a half.

He was certain that Vanora would have been able to do what they had planned in that time.

When they came into The Castle, Donald informed the Earl that the Morgans' chaise was at the door and the luggage was in it.

"Becket asked me to tell you, my Lord, that there's nothing wrong now with the wheel. It should carry the gentleman safely to where he be a-goin'."

"That is good news," the Earl commented.

"I am most grateful to you," Major Morgan said. "It's very kind of you, Neil, to have taken so much trouble and now we must be on our way."

Alice Morgan ran upstairs to put on her hat. She had not worn one when they went aboard the yacht.

She tipped the maid who had packed her luggage and the woman assured her that everything was in its place and nothing had been left behind.

When Alice came down the stairs, she was smiling happily.

"We *have* enjoyed ourselves," she said to the Earl.

"Then you must come again," the Earl smiled, "and I wish you both a good journey North."

"We hope to reach my wife's relatives by luncheon time," Major Morgan said, "but if not, I expect that there will be an inn where we can get something to eat."

"If I had known there was any question of that," the Earl replied, "I would have had a packed lunch ready for you."

The idea of having to wait for one now made the Major say quickly,

"No, no of course not! I am certain that we will do the journey in good time and our hosts will be expecting us."

He shook hands with the Earl.

Taking the reins from the groom he drove off.

The Earl watched them go up the drive with a sense of relief.

They had left without any trouble or any questions asked.

He was certain that Vanora would now have his treasures waiting for him.

"I think that her Ladyship wants a word with you, my Lord," Donald said.

"Tell her Ladyship I will come and see her as soon as I possibly can," the Earl replied. "At the moment I have something important to do."

He walked from the hall as he spoke and down the passage that led to the library.

He paused and then opened the door, feeling half-afraid that something might have happened and Miss Bruce would not be there.

As he entered the library, she rose from the writing desk where she had been sitting and ran towards him.

"Have they gone?" she asked with a touch of fear in her voice.

The Earl closed the door behind him.

"They have gone," he said, "and they did not have the slightest idea that anything was happening behind their backs, if in fact it did?"

"Of course it did," Vanora replied. "The portrait is waiting for you to lift onto the mantelpiece."

She indicated the Holbein with her hand.

Then she said.

"When you have done it, I have a surprise for you."

The Earl smiled.

"I know what that is."

He walked over to the fireplace and picked up the portrait by Holbein.

He put it back where it had been before.

He found it difficult to realise how satisfactorily it had all worked out and that he had not lost one of the most important pictures The Castle possessed.

While he was doing this, Vanora pulled out several books from the bottom shelf and put them on the floor.

Then she brought out the Shakespeare *First Folio* and the Chaucer.

She had one in each hand and held them out to the Earl.

He looked, not at them, but at her.

He put his arms around her and drew her against him.

He looked down at her and at the excitement in her beautiful eyes.

Then his lips were on hers.

He kissed her gently at first, then possessively, as if he could not help himself.

It was impossible to express in words what he felt.

Still holding the books in her hands, Vanora felt as if the sky had suddenly opened.

A brilliant light came down and enveloped them.

She had never been kissed before.

Yet this was as wonderful as she had expected it to be, and so much more.

She felt her whole body melt into the Earl's.

As he kissed Vanora and carried on kissing her, she thought that they had somehow flown up into the sky and were surrounded by stars.

Only when they were both breathless did the Earl raise his head and say,

"How can you make me feel like this? How can you be so wonderful, so incredible and so different from anyone I have ever known?"

He did not wait for an answer, but kissed her again.

It seemed a very long time before she managed to whisper in a voice he could hardly hear,

"I love you, I love you – but I did not know that love could be so marvellous."

"That is what I feel," the Earl said, "and I cannot believe it has happened to me after all these years of being deceived, disillusioned and tricked."

Vanora would have spoken again, but the Earl held her lips captive.

He kissed her until the books she was still holding became too heavy.

The one by Chaucer fell to the floor with a crash.

As if with surprise because he had not realised that the book was there, the Earl turned to look at it.

"We must be careful," Vanora said. "We must not damage it after all – we have been through to save it."

"It is just impossible for me to think about anything except you," the Earl said. "I knew from the first moment I saw you that something strange was happening inside me. I know now it was because you were taking my heart. I have never given it to anyone else."

"How can you possibly say anything so wonderful and so perfect?" Vanora asked.

"That is what you are," the Earl said, "and I love you, my darling, as I have never loved any woman before. I thought it was impossible to find the perfection I wanted until I saw you."

"Suppose it had never happened," she whispered.

"Then I should have felt incomplete for the rest of my life."

He kissed her very gently, before he asked,

"How soon will you marry me, my precious one, because I cannot live without you?"

It was then that Vanora awoke to reality.

She remembered who she was and why she was here.

For a moment she could only look up at the Earl.

Then she gave a little cry before she hid her face against his shoulder.

CHAPTER SEVEN

The Earl suddenly became aware that Vanora was trembling all over.

He took the *First Folio* from her and placed it very carefully on the nearest armchair.

Then he put his arms round her and held her very close.

"I am waiting for an answer, my darling," he said.

For a moment there was no reply.

Then, in a sobbing little voice that he could hardly hear, Vanora whispered,

"I love you – but I cannot marry you."

The Earl was astonished.

It had never occurred to him that any woman he asked to be his wife would ever refuse him.

Certainly not the woman he now held in his arms.

He knew that she loved him as he had never been loved before.

"I just don't understand," he said. "What is wrong? What are you saying to me?"

Vanora did not answer and he realised that she was crying.

Very gently he put his fingers under her chin and turned her face up to his.

He saw that her eyes were filled with tears and they were running down her cheeks.

"My precious, my wonderful one, tell me, what has happened? What have I said to make you cry like this?"

"I cannot – marry you," Vanora murmured again.

"Why ever not?" the Earl asked. "What can prevent you? You cannot be married or is there another man?"

"It is nothing – like that. It is just impossible – and when you know who I am you will not *want* to marry me."

The Earl bent his head and kissed her.

It was a long, possessive, passionate kiss.

When he could speak again, he said,

"Whoever you are and whatever you have done, I cannot lose you. You belong to me, you are mine!"

The way he spoke made the tears come faster into Vanora's eyes and she tried to hide her face against his shoulder.

The Earl, however, prevented her from doing so by holding her a little way from him.

"Now tell me," he said very gently, "what has upset you. I cannot believe that anything you have done could separate us and nothing, my darling, nothing in this whole wide world, will stop me from loving you."

"I cannot be sure of – that."

"I swear it," the Earl said. "Now tell me this terrible secret which is making you cry."

Vanora closed her eyes for a moment and it was with the utmost difficulty that she forced herself to speak.

She felt that she was dealing herself a death blow.

Whatever the Earl might say when he finally knew the truth, he would leave her.

"My name," she managed at last to whisper, "is not – Bruce."

"Then what is it?" he asked a little impatiently.

Once again Vanora closed her eyes.

She could not bear to see the expression on his face when he heard the truth.

"I am – Vanora McKyle."

As she spoke, her whole body stiffened.

She waited for the Earl to take his arms away and perhaps walk out of the library.

Again there was silence before he said,

"What is wrong with that?"

Vanora opened her eyes.

"I said – 'McKyle'," she managed to stammer.

"I know," the Earl replied. "They are the Clan on the Aulay and I think my father had some trouble with their Chieftain ages ago."

Vanora made a small sound of surprise before she said,

"There was a feud – which has gone on for a long time. I really came to The Castle to try – to take back the Stone your father took from us."

"A Stone!" the Earl exclaimed.

Then before Vanora could speak he added,

"Oh, I know what you mean. It was years ago, but I heard my father say that he had taught the Chieftain of the McKyles a lesson they would not forget in a hurry. I recall at the time feeling rather sorry for the Chieftain."

"*Sorry,*" Vanora gasped. "But the Clans have been made to – hate each other and the reason why I came here to The Castle was to find the Stone – and carry it back to my brother."

"So you meant to steal it?"

"Your father stole it from us first," Vanora replied. "Every McKyle Chieftain has sat on it – when he succeeds.

Your father claimed that never again would a McKyle have true power and authority because – their appointment was not valid – without the Stone."

The words seemed to tumble from her mouth, but somehow she managed to say them.

Then to her astonishment the Earl laughed.

"If that is what your brother feels, then, of course, he can have the Stone back. Quite frankly I consider it was wrong of my father to have taken it in the first place."

Vanora stared at him and he went on,

"Is that all that is making you unhappy, my darling? I would give anyone a thousand Stones rather than see you shed one tear because you thought that I might be angry."

"I thought you would hate me," Vanora murmured, "as the McKyles – have hated the MacFiles for so long."

"And that is what we must stop," the Earl said. "I want you to smile and look beautiful, my glorious, because you love me. We will send your brother a hundred Stones, if that will make him happy."

Despite herself Vanora gave a watery smile.

"He only wants the one – and I have not been able to find it."

"It must be here somewhere. I cannot believe that my father would have thrown it into the sea if it had any value."

"To the McKyles it is the most valuable thing they ever – possessed," Vanora said, "and my brother will never feel he is completely the Chieftain of the Clan – until he has it."

"Then we will find it and give it back to him," the Earl replied.

He pulled her close to him again and asked,

"Now I want an answer to my question. How soon will you marry me, my darling?"

He felt Vanora quiver.

Now it was not with fear.

"How can I – marry you?" she asked desperately. "If I do, my brother will throw me out of the Clan and the hatred – between the McKyles and the MacFiles will be worse than ever."

The Earl touched her forehead with his lips.

"This, my sweet, is where you and I have to use our brains. I understand now why this stupid feud has gone on for so long. I think that between us we will find a way to end it."

"How can we possibly – do that?" Vanora asked. "I am sure Ewen will never forgive me – if I married you."

"Which I intend you to do," the Earl said firmly. "But, as I don't want you to be upset and I want my Clan to receive you with open arms, we have to be very astute."

"But how? And what – can we do?" Vanora asked no less desperately.

"I think the first thing is to find the Stone."

"But you don't know – where it is."

He shook his head.

"I have not seen it since I was about six or seven years old. I do remember my father bringing it back to The Castle in triumph when he must have taken it from your father after a battle between the Clans."

"Where could he – have put it?"

"That is what we are going to find out. The person most likely to know is Donald, who has been here longer than any other servant."

He looked at her.

He thought, even with tears still on her cheeks, that she looked even lovelier than she had before.

"I worship and adore you," he said, "and even if we have to move mountains and turn back the sea, we will be married and be blissfully happy and then make our Clans feel the same."

"How is that – possible?" Vanora asked.

He was speaking very sincerely and his eyes were filled with love.

She felt that the clouds were now moving away and somehow the sunshine was percolating through.

"There is no time to be lost," the Earl said firmly. "Let's go and find Donald."

He took her hand in his and would have pulled her towards the door.

Only as she started walking beside him did she give a sudden cry,

"The books!" she exclaimed. "We just cannot leave them lying here unprotected!"

"They can wait," the Earl insisted. "For the moment the Stone is far more important than Shakespeare, Chaucer or anyone else, because it concerns *you*."

Vanora would still have protested, but he took her out of the library and along the passage that led to the hall.

They did not speak as they went, but Vanora wiped her eyes with her handkerchief. She hoped that the Earl would still think she was looking pretty.

When they reached the hall, there were only two footmen on duty.

"Where is Donald?" the Earl asked.

"He be in the dinin' room, my Lord."

Without saying anything, the Earl took Vanora up the stairs and into the dining room.

Donald, wearing a dark green apron and in his shirtsleeves, was arranging the silver on the sideboard.

He turned round enquiringly as they walked in.

"We are now looking, Donald," the Earl said, "for a Stone I understand belonged to the McKyle Clan. Have you any idea where it is?"

"Of course, my Lord," Donald replied.

He put down the piece of silver he was holding and walked across the room to the table.

When he reached the chair at the head of the table, where the Earl always sat as his father had before him, he bent down.

He drew from the seat of the chair a deep satin cushion.

As he did so, Vanora gave a gasp.

Underneath it was the Stone of the McKyles, which they treasured as if it was sacred.

"I remembers, my Lord," Donald said, "that his Lordship, your father, said that were the right place for it!"

Looking down at it, Vanora realised that at least the Stone had come to no harm.

Made of marble it was engraved with the insignia of the Clan and ornamented in colour.

"Take the Stone out," The Earl said to Donald, "and have it cleaned. I will tell you what I want done with it later."

"Very good, my Lord."

The Earl then took Vanora to the Chieftain's room, where he knew there would be none of the house party.

When they went into the room with its stags' heads and fine pictures, the sun was pouring through the window and it turned everything to gold.

The Earl closed the door behind him and then took Vanora into his arms.

"Now I will tell you, my darling," he said, "what we are going to do. I have a plan and I hope, when you hear it, that you will think it a clever one."

"All I want," Vanora sighed, "is to give the Stone back to the McKyles."

"All I want," the Earl murmured, "is you."

Then he was kissing her and there was no chance of her answering.

The sheer wonder of his kisses seemed linked with the sunshine and the sound of the birds in the garden.

They were together and it was impossible to think that anything else was of any consequence.

*

Ewen McKyle had just sat down to luncheon when the door opened.

To his astonishment his sister walked in.

"Vanora!" he exclaimed. "You are back! I was not expecting you."

"I have just arrived," Vanora said, "and I hoped that you would be alone."

"Everyone staying here is fishing," Ewen replied. "But why are you here? And why did you not get in touch with the man who was waiting every night in the wood for your instructions?"

"I had nothing to tell him," she said, sitting down at the table. "Now I have some news and thought it essential that I should bring it to you myself."

"News! What news?" Ewen asked her. "Have you found the Stone?"

"I have indeed found it and it is being returned to you tomorrow."

Her brother stared at her as if he could not believe what he had heard.

"Returned?" he queried. "Why did you not bring it with you?"

"It was too heavy for one thing," Vanora replied, "and the Earl is bringing it himself."

Her brother gave a startled exclamation.

"Bringing it himself! But how can he do that and why?"

"You will find it hard to believe," Vanora said, "but the Earl had not seen the Stone for many years and had no idea that it was even in his possession."

She thought that her brother would speak and went on quickly,

"He is upset at the thought of it lying neglected in The Castle for so long and he is coming to apologise to you in person when he hands you back the Stone which means so much to our Clan."

"I find it just impossible to believe what you are saying," Ewen insisted.

"I think you will find that the Earl will explain it to you better than I can, but, as he is anxious to make this an important occasion, he asks that you have as many of the McKyle Clan present as possible.

Ewen made a sound, but did not interrupt her.

"He will present the Stone to you in front of our castle so that most of our Clan and his can be there too. I suggest that this takes place on the platform you used when the Clan made their allegiance to you."

She finished speaking.

For a moment he looked utterly bewildered.

Then he said,

"Do you swear to me that the Earl is coming here in person to hand over the Stone?"

"That is what I have told you," Vanora said, "and, as he will be bringing his pipers with him and, I believe, a great number of his Clan, so it is vital that all our people should also be present on such an auspicious occasion."

"It most certainly is!" Ewen exclaimed.

He jumped up from the table and left the room.

Vanora heard him shouting for his secretary who was responsible for any functions at their castle.

She knew that she had astonished her brother and, having galvanised him into action, she knew that he would do exactly what the Earl wanted.

'Neil is so clever and so wonderful,' she said to herself.

She wished that she could have stayed at The Castle with him.

*

Vanora woke the following morning to the sound of hammering and knew that the platform was being erected outside the McKyle Castle as she had suggested.

It did not have the sea and the garden as at Killdona Castle, but it was impressive and attractive in its own way.

Built above the river, with the moors rising behind and the river below, it was very picturesque.

In the front there was a large courtyard and the lawn sloped down to the river itself and opposite could be seen the high hills of the Strath.

Until she had been to Killdona Castle, Vanora had always thought that her own home was the most romantic and glorious castle in Scotland.

The hammering grew a little louder.

She knew that if Ewen could not eclipse the Earl in the size of his castle, he had no wish to be inferior when it came to hospitality in receiving him.

Never had he expected for one moment to meet the Earl and that he would come himself with the sacred Stone of his Clan and apologise put him on his mettle.

Ewen had been so busy yesterday afternoon and she had been aware that the servants and the Clansmen who lived nearby had all been busy too.

They had alerted as many as possible of the other members of the Clan to appear outside their castle at noon.

She was sure that a great number of them would be wanting to come, especially from the village of Aulaypool, which was less than two miles downriver.

"Does the Earl expect to stay for luncheon?" Ewen asked his sister.

"No, he will leave after the ceremony has taken place, but it would be polite to offer him a drink."

This was to be arranged in the dining room.

Ewen could still not believe that the Earl would be so friendly, but he had no wish to discuss the situation in front of his house party.

When they returned from fishing, he was careful what he said to his sister in front of them.

"What is happening?" one woman asked.

She was extremely pretty and Vanora thought that perhaps her brother would fall in love with her, as this past year he had been so busy taking his place as Chieftain he had had no time to think of women.

She had to admit that he was very good-looking and, dressed in his kilt, he was a striking figure who any woman would find attractive.

Vanora said that she was feeling tired and went to bed early.

Actually she lay awake thinking about the Earl and how much she loved him.

How was it possible that, when she least expected it, she had found him?

And in the very North of Scotland there was the man of her dreams who lived in a dream castle.

'I love him. I adore him,' she told herself over and over again.

She imagined that she could still feel his lips on hers and his arms around her.

She only hoped she had done everything that he had told her to do and that there would be no difficulties.

She also prayed fervently to God that there would be no disagreeableness when tomorrow came.

Ewen, right up to the last moment, was suspicious that perhaps the whole thing was a joke. He thought that the Earl, having told Vanora he would bring the Stone back himself, would just send it by a messenger.

Or perhaps he would refuse to part with it at all.

*

Nevertheless, wearing the sporran of the Chieftain of the McKyles and a *skean-dhu* in his sock, Ewen was waiting with a plaid over his shoulder outside his castle just before noon.

There was some satisfaction to know that his call to the Clan had been successful.

There were now several hundred assembled in the courtyard and on the lawn and the shepherds had brought their sheepdogs with them.

They were mostly men, but some of their wives had been too curious to be left behind and they had come with their children.

The platform itself was empty except for two chairs fashioned from the horns of stags and they were there in case the two Chieftains might wish to sit down.

Vanora had said that the Earl would be bringing his pipers.

Ewen had assembled his. There were four of them and they looked very colourful standing by the platform.

It was a few minutes to twelve when Vanora joined her brother.

"He should be here by now," he said to her sharply, "unless he is crying off at the last moment."

"He will not do so and, as I believe that this is a historic moment for you two men, I will wait inside."

She thought that her brother was going to protest, but, even as his lips moved, there was the first sound of the pipes coming from a distance.

Ewen was suddenly tense.

The McKyle Clansmen who had all been talking among themselves fell silent.

The sound of the pipes increased as they drew near and the McKyles could see six pipers walking side by side.

In the centre there was something being drawn on wheels and behind was the Earl on a horse and following him were four other horsemen.

Behind them were the Elders of the MacFiles in a brake drawn by four horses.

Following were as many of the Clan as the Earl had managed to summon. They had come from the estate, the fishing village and the surrounding hills.

The procession came majestically up the drive.

Now the McKyles could see that between the pipers was their Stone that they believed to be so precious.

It was in a frame of red velvet encircled with gold and it was being pushed on a trolley by four men.

As it reached the platform, there was a loud gasp of delight from the McKyle Clansmen waiting for it and, as it came to a standstill, they burst into loud applause.

The Earl dismounted and a groom took his horse.

He walked forward to meet Ewen McKyle and the crowd lapsed into silence.

The Clansmen could hear their Chieftain saying,

"Let me welcome you, my Lord, to my castle and also all those you have brought with you."

"I am delighted to be here," the Earl replied.

If Ewen was resplendent, the Earl was even more so.

His Chieftain's sporran and the Cairngorm brooch that held his plaid in place glittered in the sunshine as he moved.

The two men walked onto the platform.

The women who had come as they had no wish to miss the excitement knew they had never seen two young men who were more handsome and smarter in their kilts.

The men pushing the trolley had arranged it so that the Stone was now in the centre at the back of the platform.

The two Chieftains were standing in front of it.

Raising his voice the Earl began,

"I have come, Chieftain of the McKyles, to return to you your Stone, which was taken from you many years ago, but which until yesterday I did not realise was still in my castle. If I had known it was there, I would have done my best to see that it was returned to its rightful owner."

There was a burst of applause and, when it died down, he continued,

"I bring it now with my good wishes for a future in which our two Clans can live in peace and friendship and help each other towards a prosperity that we in this part of Scotland have not known in the past."

He paused for a moment and was aware with some satisfaction that the Clansmen were listening and several of those who were older had moved nearer the platform so as not to miss a word.

"What is important," the Earl went on, "is that we are entering a new era in the history of our country. Two years ago when King George IV came to Edinburgh, he was received with great enthusiasm both by the Scots and the English. It signalled the end of estrangement between the two countries and it set an example to us which we can only follow."

His voice rose as he added,

"We Clansmen of the North must unite and forget the animosities of the past. For ourselves, our children and our grandchildren we are creating a new Scotland which will be stronger, richer and braver than we have ever been. This can only happen if we are united and all work for the same goal."

He paused before he said very impressively,

"That is why I am asking your Chieftain to forget the past and in friendship go with us MacFiles into a future in which we shall all profit and, I hope, find happiness."

As he finished speaking, there was a huge burst of applause.

Then his pipers played one of the most ancient of the songs of Scotland.

As they did so, the men pushed the Stone forward towards Ewen McKyle.

The Earl held out his hand and Ewen took it and the two men stood locked together with the Stone between them.

It was then that both Clans applauded wildly and the women waved their handkerchiefs and the men waved their bonnets.

Then, quite obviously on the Earl's instructions, the Stone was moved to one side and he silenced the pipes.

Ewen then spoke, thanking the Earl for the return of the Stone and agreed with him in everything he suggested.

Their two Clans, the McKyles and the MacFiles would set an example of friendliness and goodwill to the other Clans in the North.

As he finished speaking, the Earl said,

"That is what I hoped you would say and to make sure that our Clans are really close, I am now asking you, Chieftain of the McKyles, for the hand of your sister in marriage."

Ewen gave a gasp of sheer astonishment.

Before he could reply, out of the castle behind them came Vanora.

She was wearing an elaborate white dress which the Earl had not seen before. It had been bought in London for a party which she had attended at Buckingham Palace.

On her head was her mother's diamond tiara and flowing over her shoulders was a Brussels lace veil that her mother had worn at her wedding.

It was quite obvious that she was dressed as a bride.

The whole company stared at her in amazement as she stepped onto the platform.

The Earl took her hand and drew her forward and then he started in the complete silence that had followed Vanora's appearance,

"Chieftain and Clansmen of the McKyle Clan and Clansmen of the MacFiles, I present my wife, Vanora, to you."

He looked at Vanora and she said,

"Ewen, my brother, Chieftain and Clansman of the McKyles and all the Clansmen of the MacFiles, this is my husband, the Earl of Glenfile."

It took even the Elders of both Clans a second or two to realise that they were now witnessing a *Marriage by Consent*.

It was completely legal in Scotland, but not used often in public.

Then the Earl raised Vanora's hand to his lips and kissed it.

As he did so, someone else stepped out of the castle behind them and onto the platform. It was the Minister from the largest and most senior Church on the Earl's land.

The Earl and Vanora turned round and knelt down in front of him.

In only a few words he joined them together in matrimony according to the Church of Scotland.

Then, in the complete silence of all those watching, he blessed them.

Only when they then rose to their feet and Vanora walked up to her brother and kissed him did the cheers ring out.

The pipers of both the Clans played *The Wedding March*.

The Earl and Vanora first of all waved to those who were cheering them and then they shook hands with all the Elders and as many of the others as they could.

It was nearly half-an-hour later before the Earl went back onto the platform.

As the pipes stopped at his command, there was silence.

"I want you to now celebrate my wedding," he said, "and I have brought with me some food which I hope the women and children will enjoy and several barrels of ale and whisky in which I will ask you to drink the health of my wife and myself."

He smiled at Vanora before he went on,

"We are now going on our honeymoon, but when we return there will be Highland Games at Killdona Castle and fireworks in the evening which I know you will all enjoy. Now may I ask the ladies present to see that the food is distributed and the gentlemen will, I am sure, not have to be asked twice to dispose of the ale and whisky!"

There were cheers at this.

Then the Earl and Vanora walked into the castle followed by Ewen.

They reached the dining room where the drinks that Vanora had asked for were waiting for them.

Only then did Ewen blurt out,

"I am just utterly and completely bewildered. How could you have done this without my having the slightest idea of what was happening?"

"You must forgive us," Vanora replied. "But I was so scared of losing Neil that I agreed at once to everything he suggested."

"I was afraid," the Earl said, "that you might have a heart of stone and forbid your sister to be my wife. Quite frankly I cannot live without her."

They looked at each other as he spoke and Ewen knew that it would be impossible for him to say anything that might spoil their happiness.

"My heart," he said, "melted when you returned what we had lost for so long."

He had put a bottle of his best champagne among the drinks, as he had thought it would be what the Earl would prefer to anything else.

He now raised his glass and wished his sister and her husband all the happiness the world could give them.

"I hoped you would say that," the Earl replied, "and before we return from our honeymoon I want you to be very kind and help my people arrange the Games. I am sure it is something you can do far better than they can. We don't expect to return until the day before they take place."

This was a plan that he had specially thought out and Vanora knew that however annoyed Ewen might be at their marriage, he would be thrilled to have a voice of authority at Killdona Castle.

"I will do my best," he said, "and do you want me to ask a number of other Clans to take part?"

"Of course," the Earl replied, "the more the merrier. And I think, if it is a success, it is an event that we should have every year."

"Splendid!" Vanora exclaimed.

"It would bring many people North to spend their money," he went on, "and it would be an encouragement to our young men to become fitter and healthier."

Ewen laughed.

"I understand the way your mind is working," he said. "You are quite right and there is not enough activity locally to encourage those who are strong to be stronger, especially when it comes to running, climbing or riding."

"It is something we must organise," the Earl said. "Now, if you will forgive us, my wife and I are going on our honeymoon. And as it is by sea, it will be impossible for anyone to communicate with us."

It was the first Vanora had heard that they were to go on the Earl's yacht.

Her eyes lit up and she slipped her hand into his and then, as the pipes began to play outside again, they said goodbye to Ewen.

They stepped into an open chaise that was waiting for them.

They had a noisy send-off with the pipes playing and all the people cheering.

The children and the younger Clansmen ran beside the carriage as it went down to the road.

Only when the horses were able to speed up did they fall behind and Vanora and the Earl waved for as long as the people could see them.

Then at last the McKyle Castle was out of sight and just ahead of them was the sea.

"We can now go aboard the yacht," the Earl said, "without stopping to talk to anyone. With any luck they should be at luncheon and have no idea we have returned."

"What about your aunt?" Vanora enquired.

"Aunt Sophie is so delighted I am to be married to anyone as charming as you. She cried with joy when I told her this morning what was happening."

"I think that my uncle will be very proud to have you as a relative," Vanora suggested.

"And I am very impressed that Lord Blairmond is now my uncle by marriage," the Earl replied.

He gave a little laugh before he added,

"Incidentally I found your family tree in one of the books in the library. I am bowled over with how important my wife is in being related to the Duke of Buccleuch and several Scottish Kings."

Vanora grinned.

"I can say the same of you. I thought in fact that you looked like a King when we were being married and that is what you will always be to me."

The Earl put his arm round her.

"And you, my precious," he said, "will be far more important because you are a Goddess or perhaps an angel come down from Heaven to look after me."

They reached the yacht without having to speak to anyone except Donald who was waiting for them.

Vanora found that the Master cabin of the yacht was now massed with white flowers.

There were lilies and roses that she knew had come from the garden and the Saloon was a picture of colour and nothing could be more romantic.

The yacht moved away from the harbour as soon as they were aboard.

They had a late but delicious luncheon cooked by the chef the Earl had brought with him from The Castle.

*

After luncheon Vanora went below to take off her wedding dress and tiara.

She was not surprised when the Earl then came into the cabin.

He was wearing the long dark robe he had worn that night when they had gone down to the library.

The Earl suggested that she took a rest and she put on one of her prettiest nightgowns.

"Neither of us had much sleep last night," he said, "and now there is no hurry as we have quite a long way to go to where we will anchor for the night."

"Where is that?" Vanora asked.

"It is a secret, my darling, and later you shall guess where you think we are."

She knew that nothing mattered, except that they were together and she was now actually his wife.

Because she loved him so much she ran to him as he came into the cabin and he put his arms around her.

"You are more beautiful every time I see you," he sighed. "I thought today, as you came onto the platform in your wedding dress, that I was marrying Aphrodite!"

His arms tightened and his voice was deep as he went on,

"Now I can only compare you to the lilies that are scenting the cabin and the stars that will be shining through the portholes at us tonight."

"How can you say such wonderful things to me?" Vanora asked.

"I think because we are both fey that we know the answer to that question. I have been searching for you for centuries, but have always been disappointed."

"I have known that you were somewhere – in the world if only I could find you," Vanora murmured.

"And now we have found each other."

He picked her up in his arms.

Gently he laid her down on the big bed that almost seemed to fill the cabin.

Taking off his robe he joined her.

The sunshine coming through the portholes seemed dazzling.

Once again Vanora felt that she was in a dream and would never wake up.

"I love – you," she whispered as the Earl pulled her close to him.

"All I keep thinking is that I am the happiest and luckiest man in the world. I feel that we have climbed the highest mountains and swum through the roughest seas to be together! But we have won! Now at last you are mine and no one can ever take you from me."

"You have made sure of that," Vanora sighed. "I don't believe anyone could be married in a more dramatic and sublime manner."

"I was terrified," the Earl asserted, "that at the last moment your brother would prevent it happening."

"It was so clever of you to ask him to arrange the Highland Games."

"He can arrange anything that he likes," the Earl replied, "as long as I can be with you and tell you over and over, my lovely one, how much I want you."

His voice had deepened even more and there was a note of passion in it.

Then, as he kissed her, Vanora knew that he was lifting her into the sky.

His kisses seemed to carry her into the sun itself.

The Earl was very gentle, but he knew that he was awakening in her just a little of the fire that consumed him.

He had found what he sought when he had felt that it was impossible.

Now he could only thank God with a sincerity that came from the very depths of his soul for bringing him the entrancing Vanora.

He knew that she would guide and inspire him as she had already done.

He would do great things for his Clan, which would set an example and vibrate through the Highlands and he would make Scotland important not only to her own people but also in the world.

He did not know how he knew this and yet his instinct told him that it was all possible and was lying just ahead of him.

He could only do it with the help and inspiration that Vanora gave him.

He knew that she would give him sons who would carry on into the next generation everything he would fight for in this.

It was all so overwhelming and at the same time so wonderful.

"I love you! God how I love you!" he whispered.

Then, as Vanora's body seemed to melt into his, they touched the stars.

As the Earl made Vanora his, the Heavens opened and they became part of the Divine.

It was Love.

The real true Love they had both been seeking and which, by the mercy of God, they had now found.